PRAISE FOR TH

"*Modern motherhood is a comedy and The Suburban Outlaw captures the chaos of marriage, parenthood and family life with an irreverent edge that will make you howl with laughter—and nod in recognition.*"

Leslie Morgan Steiner
Editor of *Mommy Wars* and author of *Crazy Love*

"*Pamela Sherman is insightful, funny and wise—traits that remind me of me.*"

Alan Zweibel
Best-selling Author, Emmy-Award winning comedy writer, original writer for Saturday Night Live and Winner of the Thurber Prize for American Humor

"*Pamela Sherman has you howling one moment and sobbing the next—all with the honesty, humor and chutzpah you'd expect from a lawyer-actress-writer-mom-community activist-over-achiever. Her courage and edginess is habit-forming. This suburban outlaw makes you want to ride with her posse forever.*"

Caleen Sinnette Jennings
Playwright and Chair, Department of Performing Arts, American University,
Winner, Kennedy Center's Fund for New American Plays

"*Through the Suburban Outlaw's wit and insight, she poignantly capture's everyday life events—that brings me to laughter and tears. She's the girl next door taking photos of life and packaging them into a beautiful album of words.*"

Mike Pappas, The Keyes Company
International Chairman, Young Presidents Organization 2007-2008

"*The Suburban Outlaw has figured out that being happy is all about how you look at the world: having a sense of gratitude and a sense of humor helps enormously. The Suburban Outlaw: Tales from the EDGE will make happy readers everywhere.*"

Cathy L. Greenberg, PhD.
> Best-selling Co-Author *Global Leadership: Next Generation* and Co-Author of internationally acclaimed, *What Happy Companies Know* *& What Happy Women Know*

"*I've witnessed Pam's career over two decades—from a Suburban Delinquent to a Suburban Outlaw. I'm so proud. Every sports fanatic should get this book for his supportive wife.*"

Dan Patrick
> Host of The Dan Patrick Show and Co-Host of NBC's *Football Night in America,* Co-Author of *The Big Show* & Senior Writer *Sports Illustrated*

"*Pam Sherman might call herself an outlaw, but she's really a suburban renaissance woman, with a terrific sense of the magic, the humor and the possibilities of life. Her essays are honest, heartfelt and fun to read. Enjoy!*"

Jeffrey Zaslow
> Co-author of the Best-selling *The Last Lecture,* Columnist and Senior Writer, *Wall Street Journal,* Winner, Will Rogers Humanitarian Award

Dear Ken + Anna —
a couple of outlaws!
Pam Sherman

The Suburban Outlaw™

Tales from the EDGE

PAM SHERMAN

New Year Publishing
Danville, California

The Suburban Outlaw™
© Copyright 2009
New Year Publishing LLC
Danville CA

ISBN 0-9799885-6-X
Library of Congress Control Number: 2009922279

Interior and cover design:
        by Val Sherer, Personalized Publishing Services
Cover photo © Norma Cornes | Dreamstime.com

To

NES

ZBS

ERS

CQS

ACKNOWLEDGEMENTS

The Suburban Outlaw columns appeared first in Gannett Company Inc.'s *Rochester Magazine* published by the *Democrat and Chronicle*, Rochester, New York. Edited by the talented Mark Liu, they were published over a four year period in the magazine. This book could not have been possible without the support and talent of both, Mark Liu, Editor and Jane Sutter, General Manager, Custom Content, as well as everyone connected with *Rochester Magazine*. I am forever grateful to Mark for his vision in seeing the potential in my life lived in a suburban cornfield.

I would not be a writer at all today, if not for Caleen Sinnette Jennings and David Hilder. Caleen, Co-author of *Pumping Josey: Life and Death in Suburbia,* who is an award-winning playwright and the Chairman of the Department of Performing Arts at American University, told me she wanted to explore the one-person play genre, and took me on a wild ride along with our incredible director David Hilder. Without the character of Josey, the Suburban Outlaw would never have been born.

If no one reads your work then are you really a writer? So thank you to readers in Rochester and beyond who have supported the Suburban Outlaw columns and blog on www.suburbanoutlaw.com and www.herrochester.com.

To David and Leslie Morris, Val Sherer, and everyone at New Year Publishing, thank you for giving birth to my new baby, this has been so much easier than my two C-sections. Also, here's to Thom Singer and serendipity!

This book is also for my Mother, who while she cringes in recognition, knows that I am laughing with her not at her.

Thanks to my fellow Suburban Outlaws, mostly, Julie, Meg, Susan, and my YPO Spouse Forum, you have encouraged me to tell *our* truths through *my* truth and allowed me to be the Suburban Outlaw representative.

I must also acknowledge those I have loved and lost, whose presence is felt in all my work: Dad, Syl, Randi, Buddy, and Cherie; your lives are part of the fabric of my life.

This book would not be possible without the love and support of "the husband" ever present in the columns and our incredible progeny, Zachary and Eliza Sherman. The husband has been my biggest coach and supporter over my many incarnations: driving me crazy and driving me on. My entire family has been gracious and generous allowing me to air our family secrets, even going so far as making sure the truth is told both brutally and humorously.

Contents

What is a Suburban Outlaw?

In 2005, I began writing a regular bi-monthly column, *The Suburban Outlaw™*, for *Rochester Magazine*. This book is a compilation of all of the published columns.

When I first started writing, I coined the phrase that would become my moniker, The Suburban Outlaw, to characterize the many amazing people I encountered in my daily life. So, what is a Suburban Outlaw?

A Suburban Outlaw is an irreverent, honest woman (or man, for that matter) willing to live her life fully both for her family and herself. A Suburban Outlaw has a city vibe and rhythm while living a suburban life. She has a drive and an energy that goes just a little faster. Mostly, a Suburban Outlaw has an edge in the best possible way.

My husband, who hails from a really small town in upstate New York, tells me that I have an edge. Like that's a bad thing? I'm from New York City and he knew I was like this when he met me. But he married me, edge and all. Wasn't my edge what attracted him in the first place? And hasn't there been a benefit to this aspect of my personality? I mean what I say. I can find a parking spot anywhere. And I know how to get a discount for just about anything.

One day, I was strolling on the beautiful Erie Canal being "edgy" with my husband and I realized each letter stood for something positive. To have an *edge* means you: explore; dream; grow; and excite.

A Suburban Outlaw has dreams that go beyond the mundane activities that govern much of our lives. While these everyday activities may be the focus of our time, they do not reflect our inner passions. Fueled by her goals, a Suburban Outlaw continues to search for ways to learn, develop, and inspire others. But most of all, a Suburban Outlaw has the perspective to inject humor into her life—to enable her to pursue her dreams while living her "every days." That's what gives a Suburban Outlaw her edge.

My path to becoming a Suburban Outlaw was not linear and my transformation happened over a period of time and in a variety of places. I started my career as a lawyer in Washington, D.C., followed my dream to become an actor, wrote and performed a one-woman show, grew a family with my husband, and finally moved to Rochester, New York, and became The Suburban Outlaw columnist so that I could tell stories about my life in a humorous way.

I've been on this journey while folding laundry, schlepping kids, running ten thousand errands, a household, and a business, while life and death happened all around me. My road has been traveled with a sense of humor and a sense of my own failings.

I hope this book offers you a chance to see that you are not alone. There are others like you slogging through life with a dream and a healthy sense of disrespect, as well as those who want to understand the world around them and the world within them. And others, who have stories to tell, just like you. Because what are we but a compilation of our stories?

The columns are organized chronologically as printed, with the exception of the first one, *The Rebel Wears Sweater Sets*, which I wrote in September, 2006, in celebration of my first anniversary as The Suburban Outlaw.

Enjoy the ride.

Pam Sherman
January 2009

The Rebel Wears
Sweater Sets

Sub•ur•ban *(sa bûr' ben)* **adj**. *[ME under, near + urbs (gen. urbis), town] Characteristic of the suburbs or suburbanites.*

Out•law *(out' lô)* **n**. *(1) a habitual and notorious criminal who is a fugitive from the law (2) a fierce or uncontrollable horse or other animal.*

For a year now I've been writing under the moniker "the Suburban Outlaw." It's time to define who we are—with these handy, true-life examples from my life and the lives of some of my friends.

A Suburban Outlaw might miss a child's band concert to go to a drag show. A Suburban Outlaw believes that children's recitals should be banned until they learn how to play piano with two hands. A Suburban Outlaw believes in play dates only if the children are self-sufficient—any diaper changing is on someone else's dime. A Suburban Outlaw might agree to play the fortune-teller at the kids' carnival, but she'll get information on the kids beforehand so they come out of the tent really spooked.

A Suburban Outlaw's book club will officially become "Cocktail Club" when it's discovered that no one is actually reading the book.

A Suburban Outlaw will howl at perfectly manicured lawns—even her own. A Suburban Outlaw will go to a Silpada party for the wine and company, not to buy jewelry.

A Suburban Outlaw will inspire friends (and scare their friends' husbands) with subversive ideas such as "Follow your dreams." A Suburban Outlaw does not give up her entire life for the family (except when feeling really, really guilty).

If a Suburban Outlaw's neighbors put up a white picket fence in the back yard, she will: (a) smile pretty (b) knock it down with a sledgehammer or (c) put up expensive curtains and close them when it all becomes too…suburban.

When I was first asked to write a column, I chose this name with my tongue planted firmly in cheek but also as a virulent reaction to *that show*, "Desperate Housewives." Not only is the plot inane and not even close to the dearly departed "Sex In The City," but the title is misogynistic and, well, mean. One of my fellow Suburban Outlaws says, "I don't mind being called desperate, but don't you dare call me a housewife."

The stereotype of suburbia is that it's all about conformity. The reality, of course, is far more complex. And so, the oxymoronic "Suburban Outlaw" was born.

Of course, this particular one was born after some desperation. When we first moved from our garret in Manhattan to suburban Maryland, I cried for weeks. Where was the guy in the basement who fixed things when something broke? How would I roll out of bed to the corner coffee shop on Saturday mornings? And where was my personal homeless guy that I could chat with on the way to the subway?

I lamented that I had to drive everywhere and that the grocery store was way too big. I liked my little Manhattan grocery store, disgustingly grimy and small. Who cared that it was tiny? They delivered. Now I actually had to carry my own bags.

Living in a house in suburbia, I was afraid my life was all about paying taxes, moving to Florida and dying—and not necessarily in that order. We didn't even have children yet. Why, I asked my husband, did we need a lawn? But he had visions of barbecues and white picket fences. Of course, he grew up in Geneva (the one in New York). Green didn't scare him.

When I started auditioning as an actor in D.C. for roles in commercials and film, I actually had to buy an outfit to fit the producer's concept of a suburban housewife. I bought a pink sweater set that I would change into on my way to the audition. I was willing to *act* suburban, but I wouldn't actually *be* suburban.

Yes, there was a bit of urban snobbery to this, but I vowed to keep my downtown black-leather life. Smoking outside the back of theaters with the crew. Performing in late-night shows, then driving back to the cul-de-sac. Friends would say they couldn't come see me perform because the theaters were downtown and it was too far to drive. Downtown was 10 minutes away, but it was a huge divide.

When we moved to Pittsford, NY, it got worse. Not only do I have a lawn, but I also live in the middle of an old farm field. Corn is grown up the block from my house, and people buy it on the honor system. This was incomprehensible to my niece from New York City. In the thickest New Yawk accent, she said, "Aunt Pam, that is so dumb. Don't people just take the corn?" Not here, Sweetie. No corn outlaws in these parts.

I remember telling my husband as we looked for a house that I needed to be close to the city. He told me that in Rochester, everything is close to the city. I was so in denial about being a suburbanite that when the primaries were held for the mayoral election, I couldn't understand why my polling place wasn't open as I rushed to get my vote in before the kids got off the bus. My husband teased me mercilessly for that one: "The mayor is the mayor of the *City of Rochester.*"

I didn't even know that Pittsford had a mayor until I saw him in the Memorial Day parade. Yes, I will admit I waved a flag at the parade. The parade that is the pinnacle of Suburban Americana. The parade that actually had me crying as my daughter the Brownie marched behind the veterans of Pittsford. Suburbia can sometimes make you cry for the right reasons.

Perhaps I'm learning to accept my lot in suburbia because, as everyone says, "suburbia is great for the kids." The kids ride their bikes down the block to play with friends. The public parks are made for kids' sporting events and their screaming parents. The kids love to walk to the little town of Pittsford and sit on a bench and eat ice cream. (I like the ice cream, too.)

But life is not just about the kids. I have been able to make friends on the playground as well. I have been lucky to meet men and women who feed their soul with their art, their volunteering and their creative entrepreneurship. They have diverse lives studying their spiritual side, selling their artistic wares, even practicing "fashion therapy."

After many years living near green things, I will confess there are moments I think my neighbor's picket fence provides an almost perfect backdrop for the sun rising over the fields. I even find myself wearing my pink sweater set. It works for some occasions. Since moving here I've warmed to the huge grocery stores. Of course, my grocery bill has gone up exponentially. On the other hand, you don't have to make so many phone calls because you see everyone you know there.

But the whole definition of suburbia is that it's "near" the "urban." Therefore, a Suburban Outlaw will militantly stay connected to the city for any and all reasons, including parades, festivals and concerts. A Suburban Outlaw will drag the kids to every museum to enjoy the "cultah." A Suburban Outlaw will drive downtown to buy produce at the public market even though the farmer lives just up the block. A Suburban Outlaw will support the urban renaissance, recognizing that we're all part of this city and its recovery (even those without a vote in the elections).

In the meantime, if this Suburban Outlaw ever starts acting desperate and housewife-like, it's just a momentary lapse. Don't worry; I'll recover after I close the curtains, attend the month's Cocktail Club and share a laugh with my outlaw gang.

Tales from the EDGE

1

* * * * * * *

My Nanny,
My Daughter, My Wife

SEPTEMBER/OCTOBER 2005

We've just become emptier nesters. Our kids still live with us—it's not that. It's our live-in nanny who moved on.

I tried to be happy about it. "We're not losing a nanny, we're gaining a room," I told myself. We could use it as a sewing room if we wanted—even learn how to sew. My husband, thrilled to regain our privacy, took to walking around the house in his underwear.

Yet I found myself missing her terribly. Somehow, the woman I hired to help raise my children had become my surrogate daughter and, I now realized, a way for me to avoid huge changes in my own life. Which is why, after she left, the house felt too quiet and I suddenly had too much time. Who would I stay up and worry about at night? Instead of feeling relieved, I felt abandoned. It was only five years ago that, in true Dr. Seuss form, Dani the nanny came into our lives. We needed care for our young children, then 2 and 5. My husband and I lived in Washington, D.C., where we worked long and strange hours in our business and in my career as a lawyer and actress. So we wanted a live-in nanny.

Dani was from Indonesia. She had been visiting her aunt in Virginia and decided to stay to earn her green card. Desperate to find someone, we hired Dani with no reference beyond her aunt.

It could have been a disaster, but we were lucky. We quickly recognized how special Dani was: sweet, industrious, smart. Our kids were loved and safe, and our house was really clean. She taught us some Indonesian and we taught her English. Sort of. We did find her making peanut butter and jelly sandwiches with peanuts, butter and jelly. But we gained insight from each other. Dani's aunt was Baptist, she was Muslim and we were Jewish—a regular little Jerusalem right in our house. Dani celebrated Passover with us and became so proficient at setting the Seder table, she sometimes corrected me on the rules. Our son, meanwhile, asked if he could fast for a month during Ramadan. When I told him we fasted on Yom Kippur for only a day, he seemed deeply disappointed.

Over time I became totally dependent on Dani. I was able to run fast in my career because I had a great wife in Dani. An obsessively-compulsively organized wife who never complained or nagged. A better wife than my husband could claim. Did I mention she was the best folder in the world? And when she traveled with us, she didn't complain about all the museums and attractions I dragged us to, the way my husband and kids did; she said thank you.

I knew Dani had become more than a nanny when I began making excuses for her. So we had to give up our privacy for her to live with us? I knew my nanny would never be late to work. So she needed to pray five times a day? My kids needed to learn how to take care of themselves, anyway. So she couldn't drive? We would pay for private driving lessons. So she happened to crash our car while pulling out of the DMV lot for her test? It could have happened to anyone.

When the chance came to sponsor Dani and help her obtain her green card, I, of course, agreed.

But when we made plans to move to Rochester three years ago, my commitment to Dani began tipping out of balance. My husband said we could find another family in D.C. to take over the sponsorship. I wouldn't hear of it. Would we leave a daughter behind? I made us tour Rochester with Dani in mind. Was there a Citibank, a Barnes & Noble and, most of all, a Marshalls? I told my husband we needed to live close to bus stops for Dani. And we needed to find a house with a room for Dani. The house we found didn't have one, so we built one in the basement.

Then things turned upside down. Dani got excited about relocating, while I grew bitter about leaving D.C. behind. I watched her adapt seamlessly while I snubbed this new city. She couldn't drive, so she walked everywhere and lost 20 pounds; I *could* drive and I gained 20 pounds. For her, I sought out Asian markets like I was shopping for pre-schools. I drove Dani to English classes in between driving my kids to baseball and gymnastics, and I turned her on to the thrill of pedicures, waxing and facials. She would walk to her salon and health club on her days off while I was still getting my hair cut in D.C., unwilling to part with my stylist. I encouraged Dani to go out and make friends while I sat sulking in Starbucks, pining for my old friends. Dani even embraced the winter, walking with 20 feet of snow on the ground. I just sat inside and cried.

Our roles had reversed. She was an engaged citizen in our new world while I felt like an illegal alien in my new home.

My husband first acknowledged that our life was, well, nuts. Dani was now a 32-year-old woman, living in the basement, being watched over by her meddling Jewish mother. I no longer knew if I was working in order to keep my nanny, or if I had a nanny so I could continue working. Something had to change.

In the end, the answer came from outside. Two lobbyists called from D.C., offering Dani a new sponsorship that would help her earn her green card much faster than our sponsorship.

Dani moved back to D.C. in May. I'm fine. Really. The other day I was alone in the house and thought I heard Dani calling me. I jumped three feet in the air, then realized it was just the dog coughing. But I'm fine. Really. My closets are a mess and I miss her terribly. But I'm fine.

Having Dani had allowed me to travel and work all the time because I thought I had a substitute. But now, I could no longer act like a visitor in my own home. There was no substitute: I had to engage, juggle, fold.

The hardest thing was admitting my envy. She was moving back to the city I had pined for. Something happened, though, when we drove her to D.C. and said goodbye. I could fully embrace my new home. *My* new home: the one with the messy closets, and the kids who needed to be raised by their mother and father. A place where a man could walk around in his underwear if he wanted to (but that's got to stop).

I finally woke up after three years in Rochester and realized I had great work, wonderful friends and a life as interesting and cultured as D.C.—except with no traffic. Just as important, I have a local hairdresser now and have vowed to take up skiing.

When we left D.C. this last time, I finally left as a visitor to a city where I used to live. And I left behind a young woman who had blossomed, who we welcomed into our home and hearts, and who will always have a place in our family—just not in our basement anymore.

2

. . . .

Superstar:
or, I'm a Mom and
I Play One on TV

NOVEMBER/DECEMBER 2005

I've wanted to be an actor most of my life. I started out working the room—my own room. I graduated to a second-grade drama class, playing the best friend in the *Bird on Nellie's Hat*. But my wish was to be the star. I used to sit at the piano and play songs from "The Wizard of Oz" with the front door wide open, hoping that a hopelessly lost agent would discover me on the streets of Staten Island.

There were other problems. My father the gynecologist and my mother the therapist felt that being an actor was like being an axe-murderer. They told me, "Be a lawyer. It's just like being an actor."

I became a lawyer, and I can tell you: It's not like being an actor. It's like being…a lawyer.

Finally, 12 years ago, I decided to follow my dream. I started acting while still practicing law in D.C., hiding from partners who recognized me as the Murray's Steak Girl. I was

16

finally outed by *The Washington Post* when I starred in a play called "One Tit, A Dyke and Gin!" I never did get to storm into the partners' office and say, "Take this job and shove it." The job kind of shoved me when the law firm went out of business.

Being an actor in Washington, D.C., wasn't very glamorous, but I worked. Determined to be a Serious Actor, I studied first in New York and then at Oxford. I worked on legendary stages such as Ford's Theater and the Kennedy Center. I earned my bread and butter in industrial training films. I became the voice of the Food and Drug Administration. It wasn't serious Shakespeare; it was serious warnings about fecal matter on lettuce. But I worked a lot, partly because I had great suits from being a lawyer and could memorize 60 pages of dialogue in a day.

After my children were born, most often I could put them to bed and be at the theater by curtain. But even if there was a problem, I realized the show must go on. Once, at the theater, I got a call that my son had a bad case of the hives and I should meet my husband in the ER. I told my husband to give the little guy Benadryl and I would see him after the show. No understudy was going to play my part!

But I came to realize that, while I was a working actor, I wasn't becoming the star of my childhood dreams. So I found Hollywood—in Baltimore, where several shows were filmed. I was a lead in an episode of *Unsolved Mysteries* and a frustrated lawyer (I had a lot of practice) in *Homicide*. I got more recognition as the "shocked mom" (I had a lot of practice) in the movie *The Replacements* than any great theater role I toiled in obscurity to perform. I did draw the line at accepting the audition to play a corpse on *America's Most Wanted*. I have my standards. I also suffered the indignity of being rejected from a reality TV show for not being interesting enough. Through it all, I was constantly mistaken for Molly Shannon, whom I hate because she has my career. *People Magazine* did give me my 15 minutes in a profile about people who give up their careers to pursue their dreams. My mother was so proud about the magazine telling everyone I was a lawyer.

Then four years ago, my husband said we should move to New York. I was psyched—what a great move for an actor! Then he explained he meant Upstate New York.

I knew my acting universe would shrink in Rochester, so I did what every other out-of-work actor does: I wrote a one-woman show. It was produced, and I perform it continually around the country. But before that, while writing my opus with my co-writer, I got the call of a lifetime. The head of East Coast casting at CBS wanted a meeting with me. Upon moving to Rochester I had sent my headshot to a friend who was assistant to the President of CBS. Expecting nothing more than a nice note back, I was suddenly thrust into the life of a Hollywood actor.

Could I come to New York next week? Drop my entire life to meet with the head of East Coast casting? Hmmm, who will drive the kids to baseball and ballet? Who cares, I'm going to be a star.

So I flew to New York, armed with my headshot/resume, reviews (the good ones) and my dreams. I soon realized she and I were just going to have a chat. "Take a meeting." Fine, I'M GOOD AT CHATTING. We hit it off and at the end of the meeting she handed me the Holy Grail: a script for a pilot and the promise of an audition for the part of a Jewish mother (Hey, I have one of those. I *am* one of those. I can play this part).

But this was show business. By the time I flew back to New York to audition, Thelma Hopkins, half of Dawn from "Tony Orlando and…," had my part and the Jewish mother was now African American.

But the dream wasn't dead. A week later I got a call from Peter Golden (the "golden ticket"), the head of all casting for CBS.

Can I come to L.A.? Hmmm, who'll drive the kids to Hebrew School and piano lessons? They'll be fine, I'm going to be discovered.

I manipulated an end-of-the-school-year trip with the kids to Disneyland, just so I could have a half-hour meeting with Mr. Golden and not feel guilty about leaving them behind. While riding on *Mr. Toad's Wild Ride* I was taking phone calls from Peter's assistant. Leaving my kids at the La Brea Tar Pits with a babysitter, I drove to the CBS lot with my dream of stardom on my mind and an ice cream stain on my pants.

Peter was a gem. It turned out he went to school in Maine with one of my friends. We chatted about how much he missed the East Coast weather. Weather? I live in Rochester. That I could chat about! And in great Hollywood tradition: He loved me. He wanted all the CBS casting directors to meet with me. But it was hiatus.

Can I come back in July and meet them? Sure, but does he even know if I can act? Oh wait, this is Hollywood. It's not about acting. It's about chatting.

I fly back in July without the kids. They love camp and I'm hoping they won't notice I'm gone. Peter Golden's assistant's assistant has set up meetings with all the casting directors at the CBS shows. I fly into LAX late at night, rent my convertible and drive to a hotel in West Hollywood, laughing and crying with joy as my hair flies in the hot L.A. wind. I feel weird traveling without my family, like I've lost a limb. But this is my big break. They'll understand. I even see a "star" checking into my hotel—the guy who plays the dead father on "Six Feet Under." What's his name, anyway?

I've Mapquested my meetings all over L.A.—the Beach, the Valley, the Canyon. I'm the woman who got lost trying to find Target in Penfield, so I drive around white-knuckled, trying to make it around town with only an hour between my meetings, not factoring in the TRAFFIC. I maneuver around the freeway like I'm in a movie car chase. Meanwhile I'm getting cell phone calls from my 4-year-old: "I don't like chicken nuggets anymore. Can you come home?" And my 7-year-old: "Where can I find my cleats?" Don't they know I'm an ACTOR reading for the part of Angel #5? Find your own cleats.

I give great meeting. Everybody loves me. This is Hollywood. Everybody loves everybody out here. The casting directors each tell me a 40-something actress like me could take the town by storm doing parts on weekly shows: playing the cop, the murder victim, or Judge Amy's new best friend. But I live…where? New York? No, worse. Up, State, New, York? I sell it like it's an alternative life style. But in L.A., living outside L.A. isn't an alternative lifestyle. It's the kiss of death.

So the casting directors entice me with Pilot Season. "You could move out here from January through April and get an agent and… ". I fill in the rest: "be a STAR." Just then, my husband calls: "What time does ballet start on Tuesdays?" I suddenly understand I can't leave my kids for four months to maybe get a part of the secretary on a sit-com pilot that may or may not get picked up by the WB. If choice is what motherhood is all about, I realize I have no choice.

I'm driving down Sunset Boulevard to hit the beach one last time before I catch the red-eye. Suddenly my car is slammed from behind. As I pull off into a gas station, I realize I've been hit and the attacker is coming up from behind me. At least I'll have a good L.A. gang story to tell. Instead an acne-ridden teenager shakily hands me his license and his father's insurance card and tells me he'll pay for any damage. I realize that even in L.A. there are real people running real errands and red lights. It's not all actors trying to be stars or stars trying to be actors.

I sit on the tarmac at LAX, clicking my heels together to get back home to my own personal Kansas. In the end I didn't continue down the path to being plucked from obscurity. But in my obscurity I get to realize my own life-size dream: working as an artist and living way east of L.A. Here I get to play the part of a lifetime, being my kids' mom, instead of playing one on TV.

3

All Downhill from Here

It was December 16 when we moved to Rochester from Bethesda, MD. When we left Bethesda it was 62 degrees; when we arrived at midnight in Rochester it was 26 degrees. I had been transported to a parallel universe. A universe where cities compete not for the best restaurants but for who has the most snow in a contest called The Golden Snowball Award, where fleece is a fashion choice not a faux pas, and where nobody ever stops because of a little inconvenience known as a massive snowdrift.

We checked into the hotel, left the kids with our nanny and went to see the new house we'd be moving into soon. Parked sideways in the garage, with a gold ribbon around it, was a red Camaro convertible. My sweet wonderful loving generous adorable husband decided we needed a great joint 40th birthday present. He had found a used Camaro and bought it. As he stood there beaming, I started to cry—but not in the way he had hoped. A Camaro in 26-degree weather is a cruel joke when you have moved to the frozen tundra. Of course, the present came from the guy who moved his wife to Rochester in December. Consider the source.

I hadn't obsessed about the snow before we moved. I had obsessed about leaving the big city. I had obsessed about the change to my career. I even obsessed about my nanny's transition. I just never factored in the endless winter and how it defines this life in Rochester. To be fair, I was given some warning. I had called a friend of a friend, who was gracious enough to talk to me before I moved. We discussed preschools, neighborhoods and life in Rochester. I told her that right after we moved we were taking a trip to Mexico with our family for the Christmas holiday. She started to laugh an evil laugh. "Why would you do that?" she asked. "Don't you know you need to go away somewhere warm in February or April? Because you know, when it's winter here it's winter everywhere, but when it's Spring everywhere else, it's still winter here," she said, still cackling.

That first winter it didn't snow every day. Every other day. In January, right after the kids started school, we woke up to a five-inch snowfall. In Washington, D.C., a forecast of two inches sends everyone to the grocery store for milk and eggs. The schools close and children are sent home. Traffic snarls for miles. After I saw the five inches here, I called a neighbor and asked where I could hear the announcement about the school closings. She laughed at me, too: "Suit 'em up and send 'em out," was the reply. Nothing stops here. Rochestarians are resilient. They keep going. No excuses for canceling appointments.

To my team of people who help me function, I had to add the snowplow guy. People protected the name of their snowplow guy the way they guarded a good babysitter, afraid that if they gave out the name he might start coming to their house a little later. I want to know, who is leaving their house at 4:30 in the morning?

Meanwhile, I kept getting polite notes from school about the missing snow pants. I honestly didn't know what the teacher wanted. I thought, "How nice, she wants my kids to have snow pants." I never imagined she wanted them for the school day. I figured when it was snowing out the kids stayed in, as they should. Apparently not here. Every kid goes to school with snow pants so they can play in the snow. I went to seven different stores that January. They were completely sold out of snow pants. Finally, at Dick's, I found snow pants two sizes too big.

As a kid I never enjoyed the snow. When you are a chunky kid, it doesn't help to put on a snowsuit. I was always hot and sweaty in it and looked vaguely like the Stay-Puff Marshmallow man. Anyway, why would you want to play in the stuff? It just made you the wet Stay-Puff Marshmallow man. My family did go on a few ski trips to Bear Mountain. But I had the satanic ski instructor. The kind who makes you fall and figure out how to get up on your own, leaving you in the snow with hot tears turning to icicles on you bright-red face. At the age of 5, I vowed I would never ski again. I also never learned to ice skate. Weak ankles, I would say. Honestly, it's because I could never fit into those cute Dorothy Hamill outfits.

But upon moving to Rochester, my family abandoned me. While I hid inside, my children started to warm to the snow. Now that they had snow pants, they learned they could play outside for hours and the reward was hot chocolate. They could safely throw snowballs at each other without fear of reprisal: It's a snowball fight. Totally fair.

I kept watching them from the window, looking out at the alien landscape and wondering if pod people had replaced my children. In D.C., I could not get them to put on a coat.

Here they were bundled up to their eyeballs, laughing and having fun. Even my husband, who grew up here, had no problem driving everywhere in the snow. I would watch him drive away in 30-foot snowdrifts, while I was afraid to drive up the block.

I figured if I closed my eyes and counted to ten slowly, spring would come. It never did. There was no hiding behind making bread and stew. I needed to be outside, even for a little while. I think I suffered from SAD. My husband said he thought I was just sad. And that first year, since I had not prepared for February break, I realized I couldn't escape the frozen tundra. The flights were all booked. I laid on the couch and cried while the snowballs hit the back window.

Something had to change. So I bought a new car. This time a practical one. One I could drive in the winter. I, who eschewed large SUVs for years, decided to get an Acura MDX. At least I could leave the house without spiraling all over Monroe Avenue. My new car was so big that within 24 hours of bringing it home I crashed it into my own garage door, crushing the side of it like an old soda can. I hadn't even left the driveway. At this point I understood why bears hibernate.

But I wouldn't let a little accident bring me down. After I learned to drive the car, it gave me something I didn't have before: freedom. I started to go out more in the snow. With traction, I was no longer afraid of the light dusting or even the 20-inch dump. I learned to keep going. My fashion choices became dictated by the weather. I used to love wearing those cute kicky little suede boots through March in D.C., but I realized I wasn't going to wear them here past September. I bought Uggs in three colors and started to wear them everywhere, even for black-tie. Suddenly, Old Navy became the height of haute couture to me. Neiman Marcus be damned. I threw myself so enthusiastically into the snow culture I even went to Adventure Out to rent snowshoes for the whole family. The shoes came with maps of trails in various parks and an entire basket of hot chocolate. We ventured out into Mendon Ponds Park in five-degree weather. No one had informed me of the below 10-degree rule (below 10 degrees, stay inside). Our trek lasted about 5 minutes before we ran to the car.

But I knew my life had totally changed when last winter, at the age of 42, I decided to take up downhill skiing. We booked a five-day trip at Holiday Valley during the Christmas break. Winter was upon us and we were going to enjoy it.

We snuggled into a small studio at the resort, ready to make some family magic. The night before the ski camp started my heart was racing. I had visions of my ill-fated ski experience at age 5. My husband and I are not little people, and yet I found us our own extra-extra large snow pants. I was hyperventilating as I followed my husband up the Magic Carpet along with the other students—mostly five-year-olds. White-knuckled, I prepared for my meeting with the sadistic ski instructors. To my surprise, they were helpful and kind. They didn't make me fall down just to laugh at me. They helped me up. I was dizzy at the top of the bunny hill when somehow I found myself going down the hill—all the way down—upright. This was huge.

Every new milestone was a little triumph over my fears, and winter: the rope tow, the chair lift, getting off the chair lift and finally going down the intermediate bunny hill. As I gained my sea legs I realized it didn't feel cold. It felt good to be outside. I had finally earned my hot chocolate.

My 6-year-old had a much better experience than I did at her age, playing with the other little girls in pink snow-suits and making angels in the snow. And my husband and 9-year-old son went off to find a black diamond run. While the 9-year-old whizzed down the mountain, his father took off his skis and walked the three miles back to the lodge. He may be intrepid, but he's not stupid.

The best part of the five days was still the inside part, being together, playing Uno by the fire, making brownies. That ski trip taught me that I can't shut down for six months a year. Life is short enough. Now when I meet new residents of our neighborhood who have moved from Arizona, Florida and California, I don't laugh at them cruelly. I sympathetically tell them, "You'll be fine." And they will, as long as they let the snow come and don't fight it.

As a new Zen snow dweller, my transformation is complete. This year I intend to take up cross-country skiing, sledding, tobogganing and of course hot tubbing. And we've booked another ski vacation. My warm blood is now officially cold.

4

Pick an Age, Any Age

MARCH/APRIL 2006

I first realized I was getting older when I was no longer the youngest person at cocktail parties. At one party recently, a woman told me that I looked great—for 43. Suddenly I realized that the line "Wow you look great!" actually could be totally insulting. Of course the woman I was speaking to was over 30, so I think she was just being mean. Then again, I suppose when I was 32 and I met people who were in their 40s, they did seem so grown-up, so mature, so...old.

I realize now I've always fooled myself into thinking I was a different age. Kind of like dog years in reverse; now that I'm in my 40s, in my head I'm 28. In my own unscientific poll, everyone I asked who was over the age of 41 told me they felt 28 inside. It's a child's game for grown-ups: You get to imagine you're who you aren't. Its like plastic surgery only cheaper.

And everyone seems to play it. I keep hearing in the media that 40 is the new 20 and 50 is the new 30. Obviously, 80 must be the new 60 (though at that point, does it really matter?) Even Gail Sheehy, the woman who wrote *Passages*, has decided that 60 is the start of your Second Adulthood. Isn't one enough?

My husband was in such denial about getting older he didn't even realize he had lost all his hair. Working out at the gym one day, he was shocked to discover that he was the bald man he saw running on the treadmill in the mirrors in front of him. His brother, pushing 50, continues to play bruising contact basketball to prove that he is not pushing 50. Another friend evaluates other people's ages as she talks to them. Often she'll see people who she surmises are much older than she, probably in their late 50s. She's shocked when she discovers they're about her age, 48. But she keeps telling herself she doesn't look like those *other* old people.

When I was in my 20s I would do anything to pretend I was older. I wore tasteful suits and ladylike dresses. At a certain age, that switched to doing anything I could to look younger. *Sex in the City* fashions became the universal aging deterrent; people just had to dress like those four girls on the show. Today, some of my friends actually dust their hair and makeup with glitter, looking more and more like the Bratz dolls their daughters play with.

For me, it's a bit ironic, because when I was 10 my parents used to say "She's 10 going on 40." Being the youngest of four kids, I always wanted to be older. But a few years ago I turned 40—the age my mother was when I thought she was old. That number had great and mysterious powers. I had one set of friends who had to have a third baby before their 40th birthdays. Another set had to have a new set of breasts. Then there were the intrepid ones who climbed mountains or changed careers—all because of that number.

For me, the anxiety of 40 resulted in a yearlong celebration. It makes the time go faster. I was pampered and feted for having achieved nothing more than being alive. Trips to spas and lots of great dinners. Each time I went out—even six months after my actual birthday—I proclaimed it was my 40th Birthday Celebration.

I don't know why turning 40 was so scary. My dad used to say that turning a year older is so much better than the alternative. And I should know. When my husband and I were in our 30s, we lost two close contemporaries. They never got to turn 40. Now I realize how surreal that was, because at the funeral no one had gray hair. We all had young children and were supposed to watch our kids grow up together. It didn't make me feel old. In fact it made me feel too young to die. Now I look at their pictures frozen in time and I wonder what they would have looked like today.

But my true crisis of aging occurred two years ago when my father died, suddenly, at what everyone said was the too young age of 74. Unlike with the passing of my friends, I suddenly felt old. If 74 was too young to die, why did 41 feel so old? I aged exponentially overnight because a parent who knew me at birth no longer existed. While I may have been in my 20s in my own head, in my dad's mind I was always his little girl. And he could always make me feel like his little girl by just taking my face in his hands and kissing me on my forehead. I was instantly 6 again.

Also, my father had seemed ageless to me. Which is another way of saying I was in denial about his aging. He never retired from working as an Ob/gyn. I would ask him, Who would want to see you as their Doctor? You don't perform surgery and you don't deliver babies. He told me, Very old women and very young women—no one in between.

He had seen 30 patients the day he took the fall. Putting suitcases away, he fell down the ladder leading to the attic and passed away two days later.

While we all lamented his being taken too soon, now that I look back I realize that he had aged considerably in his last six months. When he arrived for his last trip here, he actually had a gray glow. Previously, he would come to our house and fix anything that needed fixing. Since we were clueless about home improvement, he took on the role of foreman with tireless energy. He treated my husband like his O.R. staff, but instead of scalpels my husband would hand him wrenches. He would hang pictures with incredible precision with something he called "a level." He used to wear out my husband, who would beg for a little respite from being the assistant handyman. But on his last visit, my dad's energy was sapped. He needed to rest in between each picture hang. I would catch him with his mouth hanging open, snoring loudly with our dog, Harpo, on his lap. The summer before my dad died, we found out that Harpo had cancer and was not going to make it. I asked my dad how we were going to tell the kids. "Oh, you'll think of something," he said. My dad died two weeks before Harpo. I keep imagining they are together, snoring on a couch, and that is my idea of heaven.

Harpo was only 6, which in dog years is 42—definitely too young to die. The other day would have been my father's 76th birthday. My mom told me that before my father died, she didn't ever feel old or think about aging. Now that he's gone, she said in her mind she feels like she's 102.

In contrast to my mother, my father-in-law shaved years off his age by changing his lifestyle after my mother-in-law died at the age of 60 after a long illness. He lost weight, sold his business, moved to Florida and traveled the world. He dated much younger women, including a fling with a 40-something.

He even joined the Israeli Army. They have a Seniors Division, where volunteers work on the bases, moving boxes. "Important, top-secret work," he told us (it was top secret because he didn't know what was in the boxes). He would call my husband up and regale him with stories of his dates. He would tell my husband he "scored." I told my husband that to my 62-year-old father-in-law, to "score" must mean she paid for dinner. It wasn't a second adulthood but a second childhood. In his mind he was 18 again. And like all adolescents, he grew up. He remarried a wonderful woman, and now that he is 82 he is starting to slow down—but just a little. He's had 22 more years of living after my mother-in-law, and he has lived every moment fully.

It's all relative. Sometimes it's appropriate to be younger than your years, to live life fully. And sometimes showing your bellybutton after the age of 40 is just wrong.

I've been told that 43 is the age of enlightenment in Buddhism. You are on top of a mountain and can see as much behind you as ahead of you. With that in mind, I'm thinking that being 43 in both body and mind is not so bad. I love my life and my work, and I look better than I've ever looked (I idealize the age of 28, but in my 20s I was chunky with big glasses and bad hair). I only hope that when I'm 50, I can remember that feeling of enlightenment and finally be the age that I am, once and for all. Let the party (parties) begin.

5

• • • • • • •

Sucker Mom

When my son took up baseball at the age of 5, the thing I appreciated most was the chance to sit in a little chair in the grass for two hours. When in life do you take the time to do that?

What really satisfied me wasn't some parental pride in my little player but the chance to make some great friends: the other ladies watching the game. And some of my fellow little-chair friends actually understood the game, which can be mighty handy when you don't even know which team you're cheering for.

You see, I am a clueless sports mother. Not only do I not understand sports, I don't particularly like them. All too often my husband would shush me for cheering wildly at a foul ball or screaming to my son to run the wrong way.

I envy those moms who can step in and coach the team in a pinch and scream with abandon at their little Michael Jordan on the field (he played on a field, right?). I often wonder if my sports dyslexia is impeding a potential Olympian.

Part of my problem is that my parents never encouraged me to participate in sports. I was a mighty good reader, but

I never ran on any field. My husband, slightly more athletic than I, once was scheduled to start a game for his high school football team—only after the first two stringers had injured themselves. His quest for glory was derailed when he broke his wrist in the cafeteria the day before the game. My kind of athletic injury: earned in a food-service scrimmage.

When our son was born and began growing beyond all the weight percentiles, his pediatrician told me tactfully, "This baby will tend toward the intellectual, so make sure he plays sports." He was 9 months old and already I had to sign him up.

I realize that sports are a necessary part of our children's lives and are good for them. But these days, to ensure they can get into college, we're schlepping Johnny and Joanie from sport to sport as soon as they can walk. For parents driving to so many sports activities, a social life has to revolve around their kids' sports. Without those team parties, tournaments and overnights at lovely motels with indoor pools, they might not ever get out.

I understand turning the sporting event into the new happy hour. And it certainly beats watching the game, which, I must confess, always felt like watching paint dry. And I know I'm not alone in this. I have heard countless mothers complain about interminably long baseball games, soccer games in the pouring rain, freezing-cold rinks all winter. One friend told me she wins the prize: sitting for hours on end by humid indoor pools so her daughter can swim for all of 30 seconds. It's the hurry-up-and-wait sport. And it's a killer on her hair, she says. After two hours and 30 seconds in all that humidity, she says her head looks like the Bride of Frankenstein's.

Yet we endure. My true test came when my son became obsessed with Tae Kwon Do while we were still living in

Washington, D.C. And all because I had a broken vacuum cleaner.

My son had attended a friend's birthday party held at a Tae Kwon Do school. They made him try a somersault and like any Sherman, the idea of rolling over on his head made him run screaming from the room (we have very large heads).

But six months later he was 4 1/2 (much more mature) and the vacuum cleaner repair store was next to a different Tae Kwon Do school where somersaults were not part of the curriculum. He begged to try it while we waited for the vacuum cleaner belt to be changed.

Right then and there he embarked on his new quest: to earn a black belt by the time he was 8. This incredible dedication to a sport blew me away. Where did it come from? But for the fact that he looked like a mini version of my husband, I would have sworn he had been switched at birth.

I suppose I should be grateful that the Tae Kwon Do studio was convenient to much of my shopping world. I even switched my dry cleaner to one closer to Tae Kwon Do. Twice a week we went to the studio, so twice a week I ran errands while my son moved closer to his goal, belt by belt. His teacher reminded me of a commandant at a prison camp, but my son loved it.

When we moved to Rochester he was half way to his goal, but he wouldn't give up the dream. I cringed every time he had to spar with someone larger than him (he could be hurt) or smaller than him (he could hurt someone). But I drove him to his new Tae Kwon Do school with the same dedication that he approached the sport. We never missed our regular Tuesdays or Thursdays. Snow, wind, sleet, even beautiful sunny days, we made it to our class.

And every three months, the whole family sat through his tests for higher and higher belt colors. These tests took at least four hours. I struggled to keep his little sister entertained, but I sat through those tests. Not understanding a thing he was required to do, I sat through those tests. Bored out of my mind sometimes, I sat through those tests.

Finally his black-belt test arrived. This test would take about eight hours.

My son finished his regimented pattern of moves, called a poomse, flawlessly. And he sparred with a big guy and didn't run away. Then they brought out the wood. Wood for my 8-year-old son to break with his bare hands and feet. In class he had broken many a plastic board, but I figured that the teachers held them a special way so all the kids could break them. For this test, they brought out the kind of wood they use to build houses.

Most of the time I would read a magazine or talk on the phone while waiting. But now I was transported into the ring with my son.

The teachers didn't give him just one piece of wood. They brought four stacks for him to break in a row—did I mention with his bare hands and feet?

One, two, three, four, he did it quickly, with precision. And he didn't scream "Ow!" (which, incidentally, he does if he stubs his toe on the carpet in our house). My husband and I stood crying in the stands. For this moment, I didn't feel stupid cheering loudly.

A few months later, my son received his black belt in a special ceremony where he was required to give a speech about his Tae Kwon Do experience and to hand out a rose to the person who helped him the most on his journey. I puffed up my chest as I awaited my rose. Then my son said, "I hope you don't mind but I'm giving the rose to Dad."

Dad? Yes, I *do* mind. Doesn't my son understand that he has a sports life only because I have a driver's license? I wanted to tell him, "I don't even understand Tae Kwon Do—but I get you there. It costs more than my health club—but I get you there. I don't even like Tae Kwon Do—but I get you there. Doesn't that mean I get the rose?"

Apparently not. His father, you see, started taking Tae Kwon Do with him, and his father is slowly earning his own belts.

I might not have understood sports, but I understood losing.

Then, after the official ceremony was over, my sweet boy came up to me with a surprise extra rose and hugged me around the neck.

When we got home, as he went up to bed, my son said, "I feel really proud of myself for getting my black belt." And in that moment I understood why sports are a good thing and why I do all that driving.

Maybe I'll never understand the nuances of the game or the rules of sparring, and there still will be times when I wish I actually were watching paint dry. But I do understand world champion dreams, attaining goals and making friends for life on the playing field. And I realize that to my son it's not whether I understand the game, it's that I'm there for him when he plays it. My son's dedication to his goal taught me something about strength and courage, and for that I would drive him anywhere.

In fact, some of our best bonding time happens when he's looking at the back of my head in the car. In contrast, my daughter is a girl after my own heart. Now that she has started playing sports, she likes to stand on the soccer field and ask the other little girls where they got their outfits while the ball rolls right by her.

As for my son's team sports, now that I have learned to understand baseball and grown to like it (just a little), my son had the nerve to switch to lacrosse. This is a very nervewracking sport with boys playing with very big sticks right near my little darling's very big head.

I suppose it's not all bad. I get to meet a whole new set of friends. Hopefully they're good at explaining rules.

6

* * * * * *

Fear and Loathing in a Bathing Suit

JULY/AUGUST 2006

Most of my adult life has been spent on diets. I am a card-carrying Lifetime Member of Weight Watchers. Earned at the age of 15, no less. I've been on the Grapefruit Diet, the Scarsdale Diet and the Cabbage Soup Diet—sometimes in the same week. My favorite period was the Atkins/South Beach/ Suzanne Somers period (kind of like Picasso's blue period). I was so confused. I didn't know whether I was supposed to eat lots of "bad" protein, a medium-sized amount of "good" protein, or no protein but lots of carrots.

Most of the diets I've been on required that I either cut out a major portion of the food pyramid or that I go into crazy starvation mode. Somehow I managed to turn Weight Watchers, the most sensible diet of the lot, into a crash diet. At Weight Watchers I learned that I could basically eat anything as long as it was portioned-controlled and I wrote it down. So I wrote down all 10 of the Weight Watcher Toffee Ice Cream Chocolate Pops I ate one day in lieu of any other portion-controlled food like fruits and vegetables.

I realize that one reason I have been on all these desperate diets is because my perception of beauty has always been synonymous with skinny. "Oh, she's so pretty" really means, "She's a size 2."

Maybe I just didn't have enough children. Have you noticed that every woman with four kids is incredibly thin? Maybe they don't have time to eat. Or they are running around after too many children. They should call it The Large-Family Diet (this is one of the few diets I'm not willing to try).

Body image is best examined through the lens of summer bathing suit season. In March, I was traveling to Binghamton with my son's Odyssey of the Mind team. There was an indoor swimming pool, which the kids were thrilled to swim in. But all the mothers said to me, "THERE IS NO WAY I'M PUTTING ON A BATHING SUIT IN MARCH." This didn't make much sense to me. Who was going to be looking at us at the Binghamton Courtyard Marriott? The gorgeous pool boys? By summertime, will we feel any better about putting on a bathing suit? For some of us, no way. We will sit around the pool in our street clothes even when it's 90 degrees. Because, let's face it, almost everyone looks better with material around their thighs and butts. Unless of course you're Christy Brinkley. And she, I believe, is officially a freak of nature. Although, she gets help from the magic of retouching. Perhaps Christy Brinkley doesn't even look like Christy Brinkley without the benefit of trick photography. The Airbrush Diet.

Our body image is dependent on where we are. Perhaps in Binghamton, we old Moms would be considered "hot." A friend of mine was sitting in South Beach surrounded by beautiful young women in their g-string bikinis when she said, "I am so much better looking in Rochester." Well of course.

For a long time I worked out during the Silver Sneakers hour at the health club. I decided I was the best-looking woman there mainly because I had about 30 years on the old broads.

Our body image also changes with what we wear. When I was in high school, my mother lamented that I would have to be (and I quote) "rolled down the aisle" at my sister's wedding. It wasn't that I was that big; it was just the awful dress my sister picked. Certain body types do not look good in layers of white ruffles—accessorized with parasols, no less. Of *course* I was going to look like a big, white, fluffy sausage. My favorite TV show, "What Not to Wear," takes plus-size women and turns them into fashion models just by putting them in pants with a zipper.

My own body image is tied into the numbers on the outfits, not necessarily how I look in them. That works great for kids. If my 7-year-old daughter wears clothing labeled "Ages 10/12," she feels cool and grown-up. But to me, a 10/12 means I don't fit into my 6/8's anymore.

I understand that wearing double digits is not such a big deal at my age. I have never been a size 4 (maybe when I was 4), so I can't lament the loss of it. But in my head, certain sizes are "bad." How many people have a clothing store full of sizes in their closets for "just in case?" I recently went through my closet and packed up my fantasy clothes—the ones I bought, hoping I could fit into them, or the ones I saved in case I ever needed them.

It seemed like the time to purge clothing because I've gained 20 pounds since moving to Rochester in 2001. That is officially five pounds per year. And it's not as if I've been eating the famous Rochester "Garbage Plate."

Yet even though I weigh more than I weighed when I got married (always the benchmark), everyone keeps telling me how great I look. Perhaps it's because last year I became blonde (it was so much easier than actually losing 10 pounds). People I know stopped me on the street and said, "Something is different about you…Have you lost weight?" Okay, I thought, I'll go with this. Blondes must be thinner; therefore I must have lost weight. My husband felt like he was living with another woman. Then I asked him to take out the garbage and he realized that under all that peroxide I was still the same. Still, I've started to believe those people who thought I had lost weight. It's the best diet I've ever been on.

The thing is, 20 pounds ago, I thought I was fat. I would go on the scale and hyperventilate over gaining 2 or 3 pounds, which invariably occurred over the weekend or at certain times of the month. Why didn't I realize then how great I looked? Because I couldn't. My body image was caught up in numbers on a scale, numbers on the labels and fantasies of how I should look.

Today, I'm just happy to be clinging to a clothing size I can accept. I can do this because certain clothing manufacturers fool me into submission. We all know those manufacturers who make their clothes with more material or with that fabulous stretchy miracle fabric that somehow squeezes my size 12 thighs into a size 10 pair of pants. They own me.

I have a friend who is constantly complaining about the 10 pounds she always has to lose. Recently she went to the doctor, who told her she really didn't want to lose the 10 pounds because she would need a whole new wardrobe and her face would look too thin. (And worse, I told her, what she had left of her breasts might also shrink away.) Her doctor gave her permission to be the size she is. I am switching to this doctor.

The other day, my 7-year-old came to me and said that some other girl told her she was fat. I looked at my perfectly appropriately tubular daughter and told her, "YOU ARE JUST THE RIGHT SIZE FOR YOU."

So why can't I follow my own advice? Isn't it possible that my substantial, grown-up body is JUST RIGHT FOR ME? Just like my 7-year-old, I need to realize that I can be happily zaftig (which is Yiddish for "size 12"). I certainly am healthier than I have ever been in my life. Since giving birth to my children I have become a runner, I lift weights and I practice yoga. I work out at a new health club where lots of people have beautiful bodies that they work hard to maintain. And I work out right next to them. I need to look in the mirror and be totally aware of what I am: a woman who has lived fully, given birth to two very large babies and will wear a bathing suit only when I want to go swimming. I need to tell myself that I will never ever go on another "diet" again. I should break the cycle, to be a role model for my 7–year-old daughter.

Then again, I recently saw a friend of mine who had transformed her body in the most amazing way. She was long and lean, and her face looked shiny and healthy. I begged her to tell me the name of her miracle diet. She told me she ate less and exercised more. Talk about a crazy fad diet.

7

. . . .

My Husband's Girlfriend is a Bitch

November/December 2006

They do it right under my nose. He kisses her and looks back to see if I'm there. He talks baby talk to her. He goes on and on about how adorable she is, how soft she is, even how great her breath smells. She lies on her back at his feet when he arrives home from work, waiting for him to massage her—the slut. She canoodles with my man on our matrimonial bed, all the while mocking me with her big brown eyes.

My husband is having an affair with a real bitch. Well, she's my bitch, too—our dog, Curley. Curley the bichon frise. An embarrassing little white dog for my big manly-man husband. He insists that a bichon is not a feminine dog; more like a sturdy poodle. Whatever. My big hairy man becomes jelly at the sight of this living, breathing stuffed animal.

I wouldn't mind so much except that he used to do all that cooing and snuggling with me. As our love grew more "mature," we lost some of the cute repartee and physicality that defined our early relationship. Now the baby talk, hand holding and nose rubbing is reserved for Curley. I can't keep up with his crazy nicknames for her: Shoosy, Pookie, Wookie. He used to snuggle with me to fall asleep. Now he can't fall asleep without nuzzling with the dog for at least an hour before bedtime.

To add insult to injury, the bitch thinks she's in charge. Apparently bichons were first bred to run with princesses at Versailles. This one actually thinks she *is* a princess at Versailles. We have been told that Curley has some possessive-aggressive issues. Tell me about it. When I try to pull her from my husband's embraces to put her in her crate at the end of the day, she tries to bite me. Growls and bears her teeth.

I guess she's my husband's trophy wife—except I'm still alive, taking up room in the bed. My husband tells me that Curley's love is pure love, while my love for him comes with a to-do list attached. For me, the dog is just another thing to do on my to-do list.

I should have known my husband had doggie co-dependency issues when we got our first dog, Harpo, also a bichon. Harpo was our starter child—the dog we bought to prove that we could care for another living being before conceiving a child. We treated this animal like a baby. We took Harpo to the vet with every sniffle, cut and scrape. When we had our actual baby, we worried about how our first "baby" would react. We brought home used blankets from the hospital so Harpo could get used to the scent of the interloper, who just happened to be our *son*.

We worried for nothing. They got along famously, Harpo and our boy (though we did find it odd that, when we took family walks, people would stop us to say how cute our dog was but would say nothing about our beautiful baby).

My husband even brought the dog to work with him, and everyone in the office said he was a lot nicer when Harpo was around. He was convinced the dog was good for business.

While my husband continued to equate Harpo to our children, I became acutely aware that this was, after all, a dog. Just one more responsibility in between breast-feeding and diaper-changing.

Then Harpo got sick. When the vet told us that we could do nothing for him except make him comfortable, I took to feeding him by the bottle and spoon-feeding him his medicine. I remember asking my Dad how were we going to tell the kids about Harpo's impending death. My father advised me gently, "You'll think of something."

Dad thought of something. He died suddenly, two weeks before Harpo had to be put to sleep. I actually wondered if it was providence softening the blow: My kids didn't know who to cry about, Harpo or their Pop Pop?

I decided that our dog days were over and we could move on with our lives. But everyone was moping around the house. My husband complained the house felt empty—as if two kids, a nanny and the two of us weren't enough.

So I sought out the names of breeders of bichons. I kept saying this dog wouldn't be a replacement for the beloved Harpo but another bundle of furry joy to fulfill our lives as only man's best friend can.

Little did I know that this new bundle of joy would replace not Harpo but *me*.

We sent her to doggie boot camp when she was old enough. The trainer told us, "Wow, your dog is really a little diva." I should have known; we got her from New Jersey, and she was definitely a Jersey Girl. No one told her there was room for only one diva in our house.

The trainer explained that dog training is based on the concept of the pack and that Curley needed to learn that we were the top dogs in the house. To achieve this, we needed to train her for about an hour a day. Yeah right.

The trainer also told us that we should never let her sit on the furniture and definitely not on top of us, which would only cement her ascendancy as top dog. So what does my husband do? He lets her sit on top of his big bald head. Now, her favorite spot is on top of the couch cushions so she can tease me at eye level. To counteract this and teach her who's boss, I'm supposed to straddle my legs on top of this dog and stand there for 3 minutes. Somehow I don't find the time.

While I believe I maintain myself with the various necessary beauty treatments for a woman my age, I'm certain this princess dog gets more spa treatments than I do. I get my toenails painted and immediately my husband glares at my feet. "Oh, I see what you did today," he complains. The dog gets groomed and he lights up: "Doesn't she look cute, my little Baby Cakes?!"

Apparently my husband is not the only doggie co-dependent around. A friend actually purchased a second dog so that her first dog wouldn't be lonely. Did she not remember how children react to being told they now have a sibling in the house? My friend's dog is so distraught about the new puppy that he had to be put on doggie Prozac to deal with the depression. (If only I could have taken Prozac because of how I felt about my siblings; the years of therapy I could have saved.) Medicated now, my friend's dog pants from dry mouth and has put on weight. But he is no longer "depressed."

My brother-in-law and sister-in-law got their dog the year their eldest son, Robert, went to college. They named the dog Robert Jr. ("RJ") and openly said he was a replacement for Robert. Robert "Sr." is going to need Prozac when he figures out his new sibling is a dog.

Another friend actually kisses his dog on the mouth. He claims it's cleaner than human mouths. And then there's my friend whose husband insists on sleeping with their dogs in their already too-small bed. The horses—I mean dogs— are a 150-pound Newfoundland and an 80-pound Golden Retriever. By themselves they take up more than half the bed. My friend, who is 98 pounds soaking wet, has to scrunch up on one-quarter of the mattress to make room for her 6-foot, 200-pound husband and his 230 pounds of living pillows. I asked her why she doesn't kick the dogs out of bed. She said if it came down to the dogs or her, she's pretty sure she'd have to sleep elsewhere.

Now I am not immune to the charms of our little dog Curley. She does drive me crazy jumping and barking relentlessly whenever a leaf falls outside the house or the phone rings. But she can be adorable, and she's good with our kids. She loves to lie by my side while I'm reading. And I love taking her for walks.

But she thinks everyone who comes to the house is there to see *her*. We have to stop whatever we're doing while Curley lies down on the ground and is cooed at by every guest or delivery person at the door.

Enough is enough. I've set some ground rules on how she and my husband conduct their very public affair. Curley cannot stay in our bed all night; she goes in the crate when I go to sleep. (Of course I know my husband cheats when I'm away from home). He is only allowed to use one extra nickname beyond her actual name. Baby talk is not allowed in my presence. Same with French kissing. And she doesn't get to wear my diamonds if I die before her. The little gold digger.

8

• • • • • • •

Sleep Tight—or Else

My mother told me once, "You'll sleep when you die." I think she cursed me because, ever since she said it, I haven't had a good night's sleep.

A friend says that sleep is a cruel joke once you have children. First, you can't sleep because you're pregnant. Then you can't sleep because your children are babies. Then they outgrow their cribs and they wander the night.

When they become teenagers, you can't sleep because you're worried. When they finally leave home for college and you *could* sleep, menopause hits and you can't sleep because of all the palpitations and night sweats. Once you get through menopause, they dump your grandchildren on you while they fly off to the Caribbean. The only justice to this cruel conspiracy is you know it will happen to *them* someday.

I really can't complain. My kids are relatively good sleepers. But it's only because my kids have been trained to be afraid of me in the middle of the night.

As infants, they couldn't know their only job in life was to learn how to sleep through the night. I am an overachiever, so I figured I could teach my kids how to sleep through the night *really* early. Someone gave us a book that I like to call my bible. The book taught you in five easy steps how to get your baby to sleep through the night at 12 weeks. If you could not achieve this goal, you were a LOSER who coddled and babied your baby. The book made me so anxious, I couldn't sleep.

The theory was that by teaching your children how to sleep through the night, they'd learn the valuable skill of self-soothing. You achieved this by making sure they ate no more frequently than every four hours and that they didn't fall asleep on your breast but on their own. You were required to keep track with a notebook and timer and to slap them gently if they fell asleep too soon. As a result they would be smarter and better prepared than all those other kids whose parents cuddled them and slept with them in the "family bed."

The family bed idea was from the other book a friend gave me. It said if I wanted my children to be smarter and better prepared, we had to sleep in one bed from day one. Given the choice between the two books, I picked the one where my kid didn't kick me in the head at night.

When my children finally slept through the night at about 10 weeks, I couldn't sleep because not only was my milk leaking all over my bed, but I kept checking their breathing every 20 minutes for fear they were slipping into the *big* sleep.

Later we saw in the *Wall Street Journal* that the writers of my bible were being investigated on charges of child abuse for their methods.

My kids, now 8 and 10, were born large and found their thumbs early, so presumably they would have slept through the night without the timer and the slapping.

As a result of my devotion to this book, my friends consider me the little sleep dictator. My children were strapped into their cribs until they were 3, required to nap until they were 4, and had a 7:30 p.m. bedtime until they turned 9. They also learned very early on that they were not allowed to get out of bed before 7 a.m. My theory is that my day shouldn't have to start until after 7. Mommy is really cranky if awakened in the middle of the night or before 7. And a cranky Mommy is a scary Mommy.

We gave my son a digital clock at the age of 2. I drew "7:00 AM" on a piece of paper and told him that he had to stay in bed until the clock said this number. I didn't tell him what would happen if he got out of bed sooner—that would have been cruel. The problem was that he thought he *had* to get out of bed precisely at this time, making him extremely anxious if he slept past 7.

My kids became so afraid of the consequences of waking me in the middle of the night that they wouldn't come to my side of the bed, even if they were sick. I had them trained to go to Daddy's side of the bed. Daddy is a lot nicer in the middle of the night.

Then my husband got "The Machine" and they became more afraid of him. The Machine makes him look like The Elephant Man and sound like Darth Vader. The Machine is the continuous positive airway pressure (CPAP) Machine, which stops him from snoring, saves his life every night, and most importantly, stops me from constantly hitting him awake.

Snoring, the other enemy of my sleep. My husband snores so loudly that when we stayed at my parents' lake house once, people from the other side of the lake called and asked if we could shut him up. For years he denied that he snored (why would I lie?). Finally I taped him and played it back the next morning. He could not believe the sound: a cross between a wounded rhinoceros and a bullfrog. He finally realized why he had a black-and-blue mark on his arm in the spot where I had been poking him every night for nine years.

If ever there was a machine designed to kill middle-of-the-night sex, it's the CPAP machine. And once I was really angry with my husband and I accidentally unplugged the thing. The silence was wonderful until I realized that I was suffocating my beloved. I wasn't *that* mad, so I plugged it back in.

Of course, I'm no bargain either. My dentist says I grind my teeth, so I need to wear an invisible brace to prevent my teeth from wearing down to little stubs. We make a lovely couple: Hannibal Lechter and Bugs Bunny.

After my dad died, I went through a period where I couldn't fall asleep because I was afraid I would never wake up. I got so tired, I couldn't function during the day. But I refused to take prescription drugs because I needed to operate heavy equipment all day—my car, for example.

I decided to try an ancient Ayurvedic treatment, balancing my chakras with aromatherapy. I didn't believe I had chakras, but I was promised if I did the $200 massage, sniffed the $100 essential oil and laid down with the $50 mask on my eyes, I would fall asleep. It worked because my anxiety about the bill surpassed my anxiety about falling asleep. That, and I was really tired.

Since staying asleep and falling asleep are constant issues for me, napping is an important part of the day. One friend told me that napping is the new sex. When my kids got too old to nap, I forced them to have "quiet time." This allowed me to continue my naps. The problem is if I nap ("pass out") for longer than 20 minutes, I can't sleep during the night, starting the whole frustrating cycle over again.

Napping is actually a core competency in our family. My husband is a champion napper (although he vows he is just "watching the game"). My dad could fall asleep anywhere. And my father-in-law has an unfortunate tendency to nap while driving.

My 17-year-old nephew's favorite time of day is his after-school nap. His friends call him and he has whole conversations with them while he is napping and he doesn't remember a word. Ironically, when he was a baby, my sister-in-law would have given anything for the little bugger to nap so she *could get some sleep.*

I know that many households have sleep issues. One friend's husband crawls out of bed like a Navy Seal in order not to wake his wife before her alarm goes off. Another kicked their daughter out of the family bed but allowed her to keep her mattress on the floor of their room for years. When they decided to reclaim their marital privacy, they started moving the mattress down the hall, little by little. When it finally reached the little darling's bedroom, she caught on and moved the mattress back to square one.

Meanwhile, back at our house, I've reached the age when even if I wanted to sleep I can't because I'm either too hot, too cold or I have to pee constantly.

So I've decided not to worry. I get so much done in the middle of the night, anyway, like laundry, reading, letter writing—all the things I don't have time for during the day because I'm too tired. In fact, as I write this, it's 3 a.m. Maybe I'll call my mother and ask her to take back her curse so I can get a good night's sleep. But I realize she won't answer: By now she has taken her Ambien for the night and is sleeping like a baby.

9

With Friends Like These, Who Needs...Friends

MARCH/APRIL 2007

My therapist broke up with me last month. She would say she was doing her job by telling me I was a healthy specimen who didn't need to see her anymore. I, however, took it personally.

"Am I boring you?" I asked.

"Of course not," she assured me.

I assumed I was her best patient. She listened to me. She laughed at my jokes. She never got mad at me. We had a great relationship.

Of course, it wasn't a true relationship. I knew nothing about her. It was completely one-sided, and eventually our time together had to end. My therapist was not a real friend. In fact, she was the captain of what I and my friends like to call The Team.

Team Sherman is made up of the many people who help me be me. My team roster is huge. It includes my aesthetician, my waxer (car and lip), my dog trainer and my personal trainer, my relaxing massage therapist and my therapeutic massage therapist (the one who makes me cry like a baby). It includes my hairdresser, my hair stylist (the one who blows out my hair and makes me look like Farrah Fawcett) and my manicurist.

The list grows considerably if you include my doctors (internist, allergist, dermatologist, gynecologist). At times the Team can include my favorite checkout person at the grocery store and the person who tells me about movies at Blockbuster. I include among Team Sherman the man who comes to our house to change the hard-to-reach light bulbs that my husband says he can't change and our plumber who always laughs as he pulls big globs of parsley out of the disposal.

I couldn't live without my cleaning person, the guy who fixes my computer or the guy who fixes our pinball machine (although I think we're working for *him*: He comes for hours on end and I swear he's just playing the pinball machine instead of fixing it).

Then there were the guys who taught us how to use our remote control. They came so many times I thought they were going to move in. If they *had* moved in, they could have replaced our nanny on the team when she moved away. Our nanny couldn't drive, so we had backup babysitters who could drive as part of the team (technically they were part of *her* team). After she moved, our roster of babysitters grew. Now we have different babysitters for different purposes: the overnight sitters, the only-going-to-the-store sitters and the help-with-the-homework sitters.

These team members have become my friends. They always ask how I'm doing and I spend a lot of time with them, telling them in great detail. And unlike my therapist, they're allowed to talk back. So with many of them, I know all about their lives, too. When we moved here, I knew no one. They were my only friends at first.

Some of them have even become like family—without all the baggage. My husband says I treat them better than family. I don't give holiday gifts to my siblings, but I do give them to my team. My husband, who gets his hair cut by strangers at airport barbershops, does not understand my "faux relationships." He says they are not friends but people paid to do a job. When they stop doing that job, or if they don't do it well, they need to be let go.

Well, that's all very logical. And I'm sure my therapist would agree. "I think it's time you moved on," she had said to me, effortlessly. She didn't hem and haw. She didn't lie. She didn't do it over the phone. She didn't do it in writing. She just said our time was up; go live your life.

But in my family, there is a tradition of never letting a team member go. My mother always says, "With friends and family, you have to take the good with the bad." But, my husband argues, you do not have to take the good with the bad with vendors. You only have to take the good.

He doesn't realize what I'm up against. From age 16 until I was 33, I got my haircut in New York City by a man named Walter from Vidal Sassoon. Well after I had moved away from New York, I still went to him. For years, my sister, mother and I followed Walter all over New York City even as his career changed, from swanky Vidal Sassoon to skanky apartment in the East Village. After I moved to D.C., I would fly to New York to get my hair cut, which is a nutty expensive haircut. We finally broke up because he moved to Florida and that was just too far to fly for a haircut.

My mother had a 35-year relationship with her decorator, a diminutive yet powerful woman who loved beige and decorated everyone's house with swivel chairs to make conversation easier. When her decorator died, my mother was terribly sad because she said she had lost not only a decorator but a good friend. I reminded my mother that every time the decorator came from Manhattan to our Staten Island home for lunch, she charged them by the hour and they had a huge bill just for yet another new beige item. Friends do not charge by the hour. My mother, a therapist who charges by the hour, was not convinced.

Then I got my own team and learned how hard it is to say goodbye. When I moved from Washington, D.C. after 16 years, I wasn't so worried about friend. My friends I would see again. But when would I ever see the saleswoman at that Bethesda boutique who always set aside the best outfits for me? (moving away from her *did* save me a lot of money.) On a recent trip to D.C., I went to get a facial at the place I had frequented for 15 years, only to discover it had closed. It felt like that nightmare come true: Your parents move and they don't tell you the new address.

The worst was leaving behind my hairstylist. Actually it was *his* team I missed. I went to him—after Walter moved to Florida—because as he cut my hair, one woman did my nails, another worked on my toes and a third brought the hot wax to do my upper lip and eyebrows. I wouldn't leave that chair for two hours, but when I was done, I was *done*. I knew all their stories and came to love each one of them.

Some team members, though, I was happy to leave behind. By moving to Rochester, I thought I would have a fresh start. But old habits die hard. My first two years here, I traveled to my stylist's house despite the fact that I hated her haircuts. I didn't have the heart to leave her. She was very nice and I assumed very lonely since she worked at home, and I was lonely too. She listened to my jokes but never to my plea for bangs.

Finally I cheated on her with another hairdresser who offered a salon...and other people...and magazines. I realized this brought an opportunity for personal growth. I would call my stylist and let her know, honestly and healthily, why I wasn't coming back. So I left messages for her to call me. But she never called back. Perhaps she knew I was going to break up with her. Finally I left a message on her machine, telling her it was too far to drive. *TOO FAR TO DRIVE?* Too far to drive in Rochester is Buffalo. But in the end I couldn't help it. Lying seemed the right thing to do. After all, she was my friend.

One of my actual friends writes a "Dear John" letter to let team members go. Another "takes a break." With every terrible cleaning person that comes her way, she'll say "I'm going to try this on my own" rather than say they're terrible. It's a vicious cycle, of course. One friend told me that her cleaning person broke up with *her* and she was certain he had lied to her about the reason. He told her some story about his sick mother, but my friend is sure it was because her house was too dirty from all her teenagers.

I'm so glad to have paid my therapist to teach me that you can end these "relationships" in a grown-up, well-analyzed way. I know I'll have really grown when I can actually cut a team member for being incompetent.

Now that my therapist is gone, maybe I can replace her with my hairdresser and cover my gray at the same time. But I know that my hairdresser is not a therapist and she is not my friend. No matter how friendly she is and how well she listens, I can at any time move on to another hairdresser. Or I can always move.

10

. . . .

Requiem for an Outlaw

MAY/JUNE 2007

One of my fellow Suburban Outlaws recently rode off into the sunset. Cherie fought a long, hard battle against cancer for nine years, using her six-shooter of grit and faith to combat everything that came her way. I'm sure she's doing her outlaw thing in heaven, beating the angels at tennis before corralling them into a glass of wine.

Cherie and I met at a mutual friend's cocktail party. We had both moved here from other cities. We both had left behind our chosen families—our girlfriends—and were searching for new blood. Uprooted after 16 years, I knew that my husband would be fine (he had work) and my kids would be fine (they had school). But I had to start all over again. There was an upside: Since no one knew me, people might think I was intellectual and charming.

At first, Cherie's grownup demeanor and chic hair and makeup intimidated me. I also wasn't prepared when, upon introducing herself, she mentioned she had colon cancer. We had many other differences. Her kids were older than mine. She baked like a pro and I buy my baked goods from the pros. We didn't live in the same neighborhood, nor did we attend the same church since I'm Jewish. She was an avid tennis player (she took it up *after* her diagnosis) and I play tennis as well as I ski (badly). With so little in common, I figured she would stay my friend's friend.

Plus, Cherie already had her posses. Her St. Bonaventure posse was lucky enough to have met her young. Her posse in State College, Pa., knew her when she was first diagnosed. Her prayer posse met with her every Thursday. Then there was her baseball posse, neighborhood posse and tennis posse.

Something even larger was looming. A few years before, one of my closest friends in D.C. had died suddenly at the age of 35. I was still reeling from that loss, and I didn't feel ready to become close to someone who was ill.

Still, one day we ended up going for a power walk together. I couldn't keep up with her. She walked faster than I ran. And she talked faster than she walked. I struggled behind, sweating and completely out of breath. All the while, her hair looked perfect. We talked about our kids, friends, and what it was like to be in treatment for stage IV colon cancer.

After that first walk I realized how connected we were. She operated at my speed: really fast (walking not withstanding). She laughed at all my jokes and made me laugh back at hers. We both demanded loyalty from our friends in words and deeds. But we gave as good as we expected to get it back. And most of all we both loved to DO SOMETHING—to make a difference in people's lives.

She was so compelling I decided I couldn't be afraid of befriending her. Besides, if I limited my friends to those who weren't going to die, I'd be mighty lonely.

Cherie fit cancer in between raising her children, running her household and playing competitive tennis. It was just another aspect of her life, but she used it as a springboard to motivate others. She started a foundation called Embracing Hope to raise money for cancer research. In her spare time, she wrote about her cancer in a book she published, *Glass Houses*, which brutally and honestly describes how a 36-year-old woman with three young children copes with a diagnosis of stage IV cancer and learns to live.

One day while we were walking, I told her about my involvement in the Rochester chapter of Gilda's Club, a support group for people living with cancer. My husband and I had been committed to cancer charities since his mother died of cancer at Strong Memorial Hospital 23 years ago. At Gilda's Club, men, women and children learn how to live well with cancer.

Cherie never scheduled anything on the days of her treatments, which were ongoing. But one day after her chemo, she called me and said "Let's go down there," meaning to Gilda's Club. The executive director—the sweetest, most delightful woman who was trying to strong-arm me in the sweetest, most delightful way to chair the annual gala— mentioned the event to Cherie. Cherie looked at me and said matter-of-factly, "I'll do it with you."

Great. Here is my friend with three kids, a household to manage and cancer to deal with saying she could plan and run this huge event with me in a mere nine months. I was busted. How could I say it was too much for me if it wasn't too much for her?

As hard as it was, Cherie had found a way to live well with cancer, and she wanted to share her message of hope with a larger audience. With more than 10,000 visitors a year, Gilda's Club offered her that stage.

From that day on, we were tied together in the best possible way. When Cherie ended up in the hospital a month later because the cancer had spread to her lungs, she didn't pull back from her commitment. Just three weeks after surgery in New York, she and her husband rented a limo and brought 10 couples to the Gilda's Gala kick-off party.

That year, Gilda's Gala attendance grew by more than 200 over the previous year. Guests laughed at our drag queen Joan Rivers, cried when Cherie spoke about her experience with cancer, and opened their checkbooks to double the donations to Gilda's Club that night.

After being tied at the hip for a good cause, we stayed tied at the hip for each other. We would drink wine in our backyards and talk for hours. We continued to power-walk, and now I was in good enough shape to keep up. She would call me to complain if she ever felt that her doctors were giving up on her. I told her to yell at them—and she did. Sometimes she'd desperately call me to reveal her feelings and fears in a torrent of words.

I thought the word "inspirational" was overused until I met Cherie. The thing is, she didn't set out to be inspirational. It wasn't just her fight against cancer that inspired me. It was her incredible energy, her commitment to parenting (she knew that raising her children was the best thing she would ever do) and her loving partnership with her husband. She fought for normalcy, showing you could have cancer and still be a great wife, mother and friend.

She taught me that it's OK to ask friends for help, requesting rides to her treatments or dinners for her family when she was having a rough day. She returned the favors, unasked, if you were in need. When my daughter had her tonsillectomy, just after Cherie had come out of the hospital, dinner was on my doorstep that night. Another friend told me that, when she came home from her husband's knee surgery, dinner magically showed up on her doorstep. That was three weeks before Cherie died.

Mostly, Cherie inspired me with her faith. When we met, I was a cynic and she was a true believer. She scolded me for using the Lord's name in vain, and I suddenly found myself being more respectful. We prayed with her family on Thanksgiving and said grace before meals. I told her I didn't know a lot about my religion and that there were people far more observant than I. She told me that by following my Jewish traditions (mostly involving food) and by teaching my children about their faith, I *was* being spiritual. It was *something,* she told me, and therefore special.

She did make me a believer of sorts. I believed in her and believed that she would win her battle. I was her delusional friend—the one who she could talk to about her next treatment plan and who absolutely believed it would succeed. Her hair was still beautiful, so she would be fine, right? I didn't figure that the constant morphine was not a good sign. Now I understand that I wasn't delusional: She had given me faith.

I got the call late at night in a hotel room in Tampa. I knew something was wrong just by the late hour. I sat in the bathroom to cry so I wouldn't wake my children.

I had been scheduled to pick Cherie up for a manicure when I arrived home, and there was still a message on the machine from the night before we had left for vacation. In a weak, raspy voice but still talking fast, she told me she would see me when I returned and to enjoy my children and our time together in the sun.

The night we returned home, I took my children to Temple and said the Mourner's Prayer for my Catholic friend. I found comfort in those words for perhaps the first time.

I am so glad Cherie picked me to be her friend. She chose carefully, making sure her friends were the kind of people who would treat her like a "regular" person, laughing and drinking with her at sunset. Goodbye, Outlaw. I hope the angels can keep up with you.

11

. . . .

Love Among the Ruins

July/August 2007

It shocked me when my 76-year-old mother, who had been widowed for three years, told me she wanted to date again.

She and my father had been married for more than 50 years. Their marriage was a beautiful and passionate love affair. He adored her and showered her with gifts and flowers. They would dance in the living room before they went out at night. Sometimes we would catch them making out in the hallway. They had private bets and jokes, and they often traveled alone. Sometimes we felt left out of the circle.

When my father died suddenly a few months after his 51st anniversary, I didn't think my mother would ever recover. She said to me: "Who is going to tell me that I am beautiful when I go out at night? Who will I dance with? Who will bring me my morning coffee?"

Her older brother became widowed a few months later, but it was a very different story. His marriage of over 60 years had not been so romantic. In fact, it was hard. Suddenly he was freed from a miserable situation. He promptly started dating a number of women, and six months later he called my mother to say he had found "the one," an old acquaintance.

They were married, and today he has a new lease on life at the age of 87.

Somehow this doesn't seem fair. The legacy of a miserable marriage is that when the partner dies, the other partner kicks up his or her heels; the legacy of a beautiful marriage is that you live out your life in misery.

But my mother is a tough cookie. She decided to do something about it. The first thing she did was put her profile on an Internet dating service. (This took about two weeks because for my mother to do anything on the computer is a really big deal.)

She spent a lot of time on the Website. But she began to realize that none of these men would be interested in her. The younger men were the age of her eldest son. The men her age were interested in women 20 years younger. Since she was 76, that meant finding a 96-year-old-man.

She finally went on a few dates. One man, knowing she was a therapist, kept asking her for dating advice. Another very nice man wanted to take her to the theater, but she couldn't get over the fact that he was not fully ambulatory. I reminded my mother that she had two bad hips and two bad rotator cuffs and is in constant pain from various issues. Plus they would be seated the whole time, so did it really matter?

Finally she went on a blind date with a man, who, my mother heard through the grapevine, was looking for someone smart and beautiful. But after she met him, she told me he was neither handsome nor intelligent. So how come, she asked, was he so picky? *He* was picky?

She hadn't figured out yet that no one could live up to my father and their romance. I asked my mother how she had kept things romantic for so long. She had no explanation other than to say my dad would take her breath away at the most unexpected moments. And in those moments she was transported back to the moment they fell in love.

Seeing my mother searching for a new love, I couldn't help but think about the fact that it has been 25 years since my husband and I went on our first date. Sometimes it feels like it was just yesterday that we met. Sometimes it feels like 100 years ago. He took my breath away that first moment. Now, more often than not he takes my breath away because he is so exhausting.

Perhaps because we have been together so long, people always like to ask us for the secret of a successful marriage. My husband likes to say that "it is never boring." I can't always say that. Sometimes it is very boring.

I think in our case, we just love each other. Because really, otherwise, what is the point? Marriage can be really hard and often love is the last thing you are thinking about as you rush through your everyday life. In our case, we talk more about scheduling than we do about feelings.

But still I recall that moment we met on a semester abroad in London and he sat down next to me at an opening tea. My heart actually skipped a beat. Our first date was at a disco (this was 1982) called Manhattan Lights. That night, after walking me back to my house, he went home and said to his roommate, "That is the woman I am going to marry."

Always the litigator, I still cross-examine him: "You must have said that is the 'kind' of woman I am going to marry." But he insists he used those words. I still blush when he tells the story. Because I kind of knew, too. It just felt right. I guess I didn't expect that 25 years later I would still have the keychain from Manhattan Lights—and the guy to go with it.

There's a theory that we are split beings and we need to find our other half. Somehow mine showed up in a bandana, tie-dye shirt and carpenter pants. Who knew my split being would be from Geneva, NY? I called my parents on Staten Island to say that I had met a boy (my mother swears I said "caught") from Geneva. My father, who had gone to medical school in Switzerland said, "Honey, she met a Swiss." I said "No Dad, he's from upstate New York." He said, "What do you want to date a boy from Yonkers for?"

It is actually counterintuitive that my husband and I are soul mates. We have nothing in common. He hates the theater, big cities, fancy food. I like to socialize and he loves to stay home. He walked into the Louvre and walked out after three minutes. He has never read a novel other than "Catcher in the Rye" and "Catch 22"—only books with the word "Catch" in the title. He doesn't believe in jewelry as a present, even though it's not something you believe in or not: Unlike Santa Claus, diamonds exist. And in terms of fashion sense, let's just say the carpenter pants have been replaced with sweatpants.

Despite these differences, he still takes my breath away at the most unexpected moments. Just a few months ago, when my very good friend passed away, I was home alone with the kids. My husband was in Mexico City at a business meeting. I told him not to come back for the funeral. It would have been too hard to get here. It was February in Rochester—he might as well have been traveling to the moon.

The whole day he kept calling me on his cell phone to tell me how hot it was in Mexico. Then, late that night, he called once again and said, "It is really cold here."

"Yeah, right," I said.

He told me to look out the window. He was standing in a short-sleeved shirt, next to a rental car. He had somehow managed to get a flight to Toronto, rent a car and drive home. He took me in his arms and said, "You can't go through this alone." In that instant I was transported back to the moment we met. Oh yeah, I thought. That is why I love you.

It's not only the over-the-top moments that keep us going. It's also when he makes me the most perfect omelet in the morning or when I watch him with our kids. I'm reduced to tears when he *does* give me jewelry because I know he doesn't believe in it. I tell him if he saved the receipt, he could just return the jewelry because in his case it really is the thought that counts. (He's no fool, though; he hasn't taken me up on that offer.)

In these everyday, take-your-breath-away moments, I am reminded, despite how hard the everyday can be, that one day long ago we fell in love. It's the same for other people I know. One friend's husband always fills her gas tank. One day he got in an accident, and while he was in the hospital she went to the gas station and started weeping, realizing he couldn't do it (he's fine now and back at the pump). Another friend's husband brings her coffee in the morning early enough so that it cools off for her to drink. He just does it—never asked.

And then there are bigger things, such as loyalty. My husband says he would never cheat—for moral reasons but also for practical reasons: Who needs another woman to hand out a to-do list?

Perhaps we're still together because you never know when you'll be transported back to that first instant you knew you were in love. You never know when he might take your breath away at the most unexpected moment—not because you've just screamed at him to help you bring in the groceries.

My mother told me she decided to date because not only does she want companionship, she misses those take-your-breath-away moments. Even while she's busy with work, activities and friends, it is the possibility of finding love that puts her out there.

Surprisingly, though, my dad even in passing away is still the most romantic man. After he died, my mother was looking in his drawers and found her birthday card and Valentine's card, which he had already purchased, tucked away behind his socks. And it took her breath away.

12

• • • • • • •

Odyssey Out of My Mind

September/October 2007

I'm sure something I did in a past life condemned me to attend the Odyssey of the Mind World Finals in East Lansing, Mich., and it must have been something very bad. Yes, it was a life-changing opportunity for my son, who was competing in the creative problem-solving competition for children. But for his mother, it was the Seventh Circle of Hell.

How else to explain having to stay in a dorm with seven 11-year-old boys? In a room that shook with the sound of a train running every two hours through the night. While gaining the Freshman 10 in a matter of days from all that cafeteria food. And then the really bad stuff happened.

But let me start at the beginning. "Come on," my friend said last September, "be a coach. It'll be fun." And with that I was sucked into the weird and wonderful world of Odyssey of the Mind. My friend, who had been doing this for six years, conned me into the job of co-coach with a breezy promise that it would be easy and rewarding. Liar.

I, who had never done "team" anything, would now be called "Coach." There's a reason the play I wrote and performed is a *solo* show. I vowed never to coach a child's sports team, mainly because I have no patience for my own children, let alone other people's children. I told my husband *he* should be the coach because he has this need to tell people what to do, and he loves to scream directions from the sidelines despite a staggering lack of sports knowledge.

Turns out that Odyssey of the Mind has a rule forbidding "outside assistance." This means that the coach can only act as a facilitator. At first, this worked out well for me because I honestly didn't understand what the boys had to do. And I admit I was proud that our name became Team Sherman.

The students compete by working on five different problems. The long-term portion requires them to perform a skit, build a set and make their own costumes—and they somehow have to incorporate problem-solving into their presentation. They receive points for every aspect of their performance.

Our boys picked the "Out of the Box Balsa" problem. They had to build a small structure made of balsa wood that weighed less than 18 grams. Through some miracle of physics, the structure was to be built to bear massive weight. While they performed their skit, they proceeded to place large weights on the structure until it was crushed. At their first competition, their structure held 535 pounds.

In the spontaneous portion, the students go into a room and have three minutes to solve a problem. Often it's a McGyver-like problem: Here is some gum, a rubber band and a banana: Go build a bridge.

The spontaneous portion is the great leveler. A team might secretly receive outside assistance in the long-term part, but not in spontaneous. No one is allowed to enter the room with the teams.

If you win a competition, you advance to the next level. And our little geniuses kept winning—at the regionals in February and again at the state finals in March. That sounds like a good thing, but I should have known something was up when the mothers who lost at the state finals were smiling. Another team's coach looked at me and said, "I'm so sorry." When I asked why, she explained that third place is best since that earns a trophy but not a slot in the Worlds. That's when I realized this would drag on another two months.

Before the Worlds, my co-coach took me for a walk and told me I didn't understand the concept of "no outside assistance." The boys had to sign an oath stating that they had no assistance, and one of the boys had narced on me: "Mrs. Sherman told us to use the word "ergle" to rhyme with "snurgle." I told my co-coach I simply had been singing with them to the tune of "Domo Arrigato Mr. Roboto" when I used the word. I didn't tell them to use it. Anyway, what else rhymes with snurgle? "Gurgle," she said, but I hadn't thought of that at the time.

I also had told them to speak up at one point. What's wrong with that? According to the rules, she said, a coach may ask, "What would you do if the audience can't hear the words?" And the kids have to solve that problem. Puhleeze.

But apparently it mattered. During our walk, my co-coach fired me.

I pleaded, "You can't fire me. It's called Team Sherman!"

I cursed and complained. But then I thought, What a relief! I was done! I could go back to MY LIFE.

But no, I wasn't *completely* fired. I would still have to chaperone the boys during the World Finals, sleeping in their dorm building (the Odyssey officials are okay with outside assistance that gets the kids to shower and brush their teeth).

My family drove to Michigan State University for the Finals, where 810 teams from 12 countries would compete. When my son and I walked into the dorm, a former army barracks with urinals in the ladies rooms and a sauna-like feel because of a freak heat wave, I started to cry. At my age, a bathroom down the hall is more than a small inconvenience.

Did I mention there was no liquor on campus?

Meanwhile, my husband and daughter and all the other parents stayed in an off-campus hotel, the Country Suites. He took me there at one point to take a nap in a real bed. It was the Taj Mahal.

One night, one of the boys knocked at my door at five a.m. "Mrs. Sherman, I just got sick." My co-coach managed to sleep through the pounding on the door. I cleaned it up with the mop and bucket handed to me by the snickering co-ed at the front desk.

I didn't think it could get worse. But one morning, on the way to the showers, the boys turned back and yelled, "Mrs. Sherman! Someone pooped in the shower!" I rounded up a bunch of boys, still dripping in their towels, and asked loudly, "which one of you wet boys did this?" Then it was off to the girls' showers, with me standing guard outside because the boys were terrified that a girl would walk in.

I had five days of this while the kids were in their glory, buying incredibly expensive souvenirs, rabidly trading Odyssey of the Mind pins and meeting people from all over the world. Teams had come from China, Korea, Poland and Singapore. My son even met a team from Kazakhstan. (I told him they would not find his Borat impersonation even remotely funny.)

Our team hosted the Singapore team as their "Buddy Team." The parents from Singapore couldn't believe we were volunteers. Their coach was paid. Paid?!

Since the coaches can't assist the kids, they have their own competition during the Worlds—I guess to feel useful. On the final night, there was a grown-up coach's party with—thank you—liquor, so all those pent-up coaches could cut loose. A guy in a homemade, light-bulb-shaped hat tried to pick me up as "YMCA" blared in the background.

Finally, there was the competition itself: The blessed 20 minutes we had driven all the way to Michigan for. I, for one, wasn't feeling too good. But our boys performed like a dream. They improvised when they encountered technical difficulties, worked together as a team and dealt with the pressure beautifully. Their costumes included an orange crate, a cardboard box and felt bunny ears. And they produced every bit of it on their own.

Then I watched the other teams with their just-short-of-Broadway sets, obviously tailored costumes, Las Vegas-like special effects and balsa-wood structures that held over 1,000 pounds. My mouth hung open. In my most encouraging but reality-laden coach's voice, I told the boys, "Coming to Worlds is its own reward." My son looked at me like I had betrayed him.

We gathered at the awards ceremony, awaiting the results. I realized it's not often you can sit in a stadium of 12,000 people wearing silly hats, t-shirts and pins (which some of the adults had shamelessly horded from the kids), all cheering the kids for just being smart.

Our boys were blowing the incredibly loud horns I had stupidly let them buy, while my co-coach (who had told them not to buy the horns) sat smiling at me, very peacefully, with earplugs sticking out of her ears. We started laughing hysterically, and I finally got it. I was part of a team. And I had contributed by staying in the dorm, being there every step of the way and giving them the opportunity to grow on their own.

The announcer started naming the winners. Only the top six teams in each category would be named. Our boys locked arms. I whispered to the Mom sitting next to me, "They must be delusional. They aren't going to win anything." And then they announced that our team had placed fifth in the world. Their spontaneous scores had vaulted them to the top five.

The boys screamed at the top of their lungs, but I offered my best outside assistance by screaming just as loudly.

13

• • • • • • • •

My Own, Private Manhattan

NOVEMBER/DECEMBER 2007

My vision of New York City was born at the movies. *Annie Hall, Manhattan, Breakfast at Tiffany's.* I grew up on one of the five boroughs, but it was the forgotten one—Staten Island—and we always referred to Manhattan as "The City." Everyone knew which city we were referring to.

My parents took us into the city constantly, for "cultah." My mother would say, "Aren't we lucky to live so close to the city?" And I would think, "Not close enough."

My movie version didn't reflect the real Manhattan. There were no urine-soaked alleys or homeless people on the corner. My view was drenched in sepia tones, with the sound of jazz music in the background instead of jackhammers.

After I was engaged to be married, in 1983, I was so excited that my guy from the country agreed to give Manhattan a go while I finished my last year of college. I didn't even mind when he decided to live in what was then referred to as no-man's land, Gateway Plaza, the only apartment building on the lower west side, right across from the World Trade Center. It wasn't ideal. The whole of lower Manhattan was under construction the entire time he lived there. There was one grocery store, the Red Apple, where none of the apples were red. You had to go all the way to Chelsea to get decent Chinese food. And worst of all, it was a delivery-free zone.

But I loved looking at the World Trade Center. The restaurant, Windows on the World, held special memories as the place that my parents would go for family celebrations. You would take the elevator and as it whooshed to the top you felt the building vibrate. At the top, you could see all the way to Pennsylvania.

After we got married, we moved into my sister's old apartment in the West Village. But you could still see the World Trade Center reining over lower Manhattan. Finally, after three more years of New York, my husband cried "Uncle." I believe the precise moment came when our car was melted on the street by vandals.

We moved to Washington, D.C., our compromise city, but I was still connected to The City. My family still lived on Staten Island. And my hairdresser was in New York. I worked for a large law firm that had a New York office. For a period of six months, I took the three-hour train to Penn Station and lived in a hotel overlooking Central Park. New York on an expense account; I loved it.

While I still cried that I wasn't *living* in the city, I eventually told myself I was part of a new movie, *Mrs. Sherman Goes to Washington*. Then in 2001, after 16 years in D.C., we made the decision to move to Rochester—even farther from my city— for my husband's business. We planned to be in Rochester by December 2001.

But before we moved, I wanted one last easy train ride into Manhattan, so I told my husband we needed a romantic night away. We chose September 10.

We took the train and checked into a hotel on Union Square. We specifically asked for a room high up in the hotel facing lower Manhattan because we loved the view of the World Trade Center.

We had a strange and magical evening. A friend was opening a new cabaret act, so we went to see it. Celebrities dotted the audience, including Cynthia Nixon from "Sex and the City," who I chatted with about kindergarten (our kids were the same age). We stepped out of the club into the pouring rain and a cab mysteriously appeared to swoop us up.

We drove to the Union Square Café and waited at the bar while our table was readied. Two beautifully dressed ladies were sitting at the bar next to me, and I complimented one of them on her bracelet and asked where she had purchased it. "At home, in Rochester, New York," she said. Weird. I described our impending move, and they said we would love our new city. I protested that I was being forced to move, but the ladies were so nice—and so much better dressed than Cynthia Nixon—it gave me hope. I took their phone numbers and said we would call when we got there.

Finally, we skipped back to our room and watched the glow of lower Manhattan from the window. We closed the drapes and drifted off to sleep.

And we woke up the next morning in a different kind of New York movie—this time a horror movie.

We had slept later than normal, and when the waiter came up to the room he said, "Did you hear? A plane has flown into the World Trade Center." He opened the drapes and we looked out the window. A moment later, we saw the second plane hit the building. We turned on the television and the whole world fell apart.

My husband said we had to try to get home to D.C., unaware of the plane that had flown into the Pentagon. We finally got through to our nanny who was home with our daughter and told her that she should get our son home from kindergarten and not let the kids watch TV.

We packed and went to check out. The hotel manager exhorted us to stay, as he didn't think anyone would be leaving Manhattan. But my husband was determined. We left, setting off on foot for Penn Station.

I felt safe with my big guy by my side, and I hoped for the best in the chaos of the streets. In the middle of it all, I started to worry about those two ladies from Rochester. They were staying at an apartment in the Village, but I wondered if they had been able to get home.

We dragged our luggage uptown and walked over to 5th Avenue. Suddenly everyone stopped, with mouths agape, and stared at lower Manhattan. "Don't look back," my husband said. "Keep going." But like Lot's wife, I couldn't resist. In that moment, in a cloud of dust, we saw the towers fall.

We ran into Penn Station and saw the mobs trying to get tickets. I was standing on line and started talking to a woman with a worried look on her face. She said, "I'm trying to get home to Rochester, New York." I took her card and wished her luck. And then I saw policemen start flooding the station and the ticket sellers closing down all the counters.

I pleaded with my husband to leave the station. "What if this is the next target?" And for good measure, I added,

"This will be the biggest 'I told you so' *ever* if we lose our hotel room."

We hurried back downtown and saw a flood of people walking uptown. Buses were filled with stunned people crushed together. One man, in a suit covered in gray dust, sat on a curb with his head in his hands, weeping.

Back at the hotel, the manager welcomed us back. He had been holding our room, just in case.

That night we went to find some food with my brother-in-law, who hadn't even been able to get back to Staten Island and was sleeping on our hotel-room floor. It was a beautiful late summer night in Manhattan. The sky was a vibrant blue, without a cloud in it. The restaurant was jammed with people drinking at the bar. Like any other night in Manhattan. And yet this night, we were prisoners on my beloved island, unable to get to our loved ones.

After a sleepless night, at 5 a.m., we left the hotel. We saw the National Guard setting up barriers as they closed down lower Manhattan below Union Square. Overnight, people had placed pictures of the missing on the barriers.

The conductor at Penn Station told us we could use our tickets from the day before. There was no security search as we entered the train. I spied my fellow passengers with fear, including a young man who sat in front of us with a huge package on his lap. I eyed him nervously until I overheard him talking to his bride-to-be about their upcoming wedding. Yes, he had the tuxes in that box.

As the train left Manhattan and pulled out of the underground into the bright New Jersey sky, we looked back at the smoldering holes in lower Manhattan. My fantasy city would never be the same again.

Washington, D.C., was eerily quiet. There was no air traffic, no helicopters buzzing, no flights taking off from National Airport.

We drove home, eager to see our children. As we walked into our house, I heard the TV. The kids were watching another one of my favorite movies, *The Wizard of Oz*. As we hugged our kids tight, we heard Glinda telling Dorothy that she had the power all along to go home. All she had to do was click her heels and say, "There's no place like home." My husband and I started to cry.

I called those ladies from Rochester to make sure they had gotten home safely. They had taken an early morning flight and had gotten home just fine.

In December, when we moved from D.C., people said, "Oh, you're moving up there because it's safe." But we had decided to move away before the world turned upside down.

We have been living in Rochester for six years this December. So while I'm not living in *the* City, Rochester is now *my* city. Perhaps in moving to a place that isn't the center of the universe, the universe was sending me a message. Because this city has widened my horizons in ways I never could have imagined with my New York City myopia.

Today, I am starring in a new movie of my own making, about my life lived near a cornfield. Maybe, in reality, no place is really safe. But I do know there is still no place like home.

14

· · · · · · ·

The Ties That
Bind—and Gag

JANUARY/FEBRUARY 2008

When my husband first met my family 25 years ago, he told me I was like Marilyn of "The Munsters." Marilyn, if you'll recall, was the pretty, "normal" blonde who lived with her Frankenstein uncle and vampiress aunt, Herman and Lily Munster. To the outside world she was the normal one, but inside the house she was considered odd, never quite fitting in among the crazies.

My family—the elder twin boy and girl, another brother and me (the youngest)—was seemingly normal. We did not live in a dilapidated mansion on the hill with a blood-sucking grandpa. Yet, behind closed doors, I always felt that they were all...Munsters.

I was always distancing myself from my "crazy" family. I even took to pronouncing my name differently. Once, when my father heard, he corrected me. I told him, "Oh, I don't want to be a member of *that* family."

Very little of my childhood memory involves the kinds of sibling relationships I found in the books of my youth, like

The Bobbsey Twins or *The Hardy Boys*, working cheerfully together as a team to solve a crime. Most of my sibling interactions involved yelling, pain and competing for food.

There were seven years between my eldest sister and I, so I became her personal slave. She often ignored me unless she wanted something from me or felt the need to use me as her test doll, like when she plucked my eyebrows at the age of 8 or shaved my legs way too early at the age of 6. Her twin was very entrepreneurial at a very young age. More often than not he made his money through the usury of his siblings.

My next oldest brother, when he wasn't beating me up and calling me names, would sneak into my room at night and tell me stories about an ancient Indian who lived in the walls in my room, knocking to get out. This terrified me, and every knock of our heating system made me scream.

Our fighting was legendary. The two brothers fought for years because they shared a room. There is still a dent in the wall where one of them threw a guitar stand at the other, missing the other's head by inches.

Of course, I was no innocent in all the mayhem. I would burst in on my sister and her many boyfriends, threatening to rat her out because she had her shirt off in the dark with a boy.

We all grew up to be self-sufficient, hard-working and accomplished. My sister is both a therapist (go figure) and an incredible artist. Her twin, in addition to being an executive, breeds dogs. My other brother likes to remind us that he is the busiest of all of us because he is, and I quote, "a doctor, dammit." Now we call him Dr. Dammit. Of course, he *is* a world-famous surgeon. He'll tell you so himself (I can't help but think his grateful patients would be astonished to know that he physically tortured me before he took the Hippocratic Oath).

None of our accomplishments stop us from acting like children when we get together. No matter how old I am, I am still sucked back into the role of "the baby" when I'm with them. Our relationships today, even in middle age, are still defined by how we grew up together.

Actually, I don't have to have relationships with my siblings. I don't talk to them all that often. My mother tells me everything that happens in their lives—like the town crier—with color commentary.

My mother likes to say that she is very proud that each of her children are "INDIVIDUALS." What she means is she can't quite believe we are all from the same genetic pool. One brother calls my mother five times a day. The other brother calls maybe five times a year. One brother is the family memory keeper, always recounting something embarrassing that you wish no one would remember. The other doesn't remember a thing, as if he had been mind-swiped by those "Men in Black" guys.

My sister takes my mother shopping at Prada. I take her to Marshalls. My sister tells my mother her hair looks terrible when she cuts it short. I tell her it's too long and she needs to get it cut. My poor mother is so worried she will forget which daughter likes which style and make a mistake and wear the wrong shoes and comb her hair the wrong way when she sees one of us. (I cannot believe we were raised by the same mother. I mean, PRADA? *Really*. She taught us better than to buy shoes the price of a couch.)

My mother says she would have had more children if she could. But I learned from our family. Two was plenty, especially seeing how we rocked my son's world when our daughter was born—and not in a good way. For almost three years he had been the center of the universe. And then the interloper moved in. After two weeks, he looked at me and said, "When are you taking her back to the hospital?" I replied, "Your sister lives here now." He ordered, "No. Time for her to go."

After he realized she was staying, he started using her as his personal punching bag. I sat my son down after he tried to press into that soft spot in her head one too many times and told him that we had given him the greatest gift of his life: a sibling. In other words, I lied.

I can't help but think I'm forcing a fantasy on my kids that they have to like each other. When they fight, I scream at them, "Who is your best friend?" They dutifully answer in a monotone voice, "He is." "She is." But they don't mean it. What they really mean is: Why did you bring this person into my life? And really, how can I exhort my children to get along when even at the age of 45 I still don't get along with my siblings?

And yet my husband and his brother are very close. They are five years apart. Perhaps that's the magic number because my husband knows who is in charge—his brother—and for the rest of his life, as long as he does what his brother says, things will go easy for him.

I have a friend who is incredibly close with her sister. They have some weird intuition; they'll call each other at the most needed times without prompting. Then again, her sister lives in Africa. It's easy to get along when you live half a world away.

Another friend is the youngest of 15. Yes, 15. Children. There is a 22-year difference between her and her oldest sibling. She was one when she became an aunt. When my friend turned 10, her mother looked at her (her 15th child) and sighed that she wanted to adopt another (she didn't). They all keep in touch through e-mail, family reunions and published lists of birthdays and addresses. I marvel at how they stay connected despite the sheer volume.

There are, of course, those people I know who don't ever talk to their siblings. They won't even attend family events because the other will be present. Usually something egregious has occurred and it almost always has to do with money.

And there's my mother and her older brother, 77 and 86 respectively. They talk every day. Every day he yells at her. Every day she tells him he is crazy. The other day he called just to tell her he loved her.

Last summer, my mother decided to sell her country home—my parents' "On Golden Pond" house. When my siblings and I gathered to divide the contents of the house, I thought it would be a debacle of fighting and the usual competition for stuff. But something weird happened that day. All the rivalries and childishness melted away. We were generous and gracious with each other. I kept thinking, "Who are these pod people that have replaced my siblings?"

There was a big difference in the make-up of the family. Something had shifted between my siblings when our father died. The fighting that had gone on over the years began to melt away as we each traversed the passing of our father, both as individuals and as a collective. We helped our mother transition into widowhood. We supported each other.

I realized that my siblings had changed and grown in the years since we all lived together, just as I have. Over the years, we simply grew up and became strangers. We probably wouldn't choose each other as friends, but we are stuck with each other for life. We are connected by more than just the same DNA. These people have been present at every big life event: weddings, births and at our father's gravesite. It was in that moment that I understood and appreciated having these people, these strangers, on my side. While we may not share the same interests, we share the same values and a history together. In the end they will be the people who will know me the longest in my life.

I suppose I will always feel a little like Marilyn, and not just because I am now blonde. Despite their differences, Marilyn loved her family and defended them against the town bullies.

Of course, my siblings will always treat me as their baby sister. But I've got the last laugh, because even when I'm 90, I'll *still* be younger than them all.

15

. . . .

My Husband's
Wife is a Bitch

MARCH/APRIL 2008

One woman said her husband has it scheduled into his planner so he can plan his business trips around it. Another friend discussed it with my husband a few months after getting married: "I just don't understand it—she just *burst into flames*." One man told me, "There is a reason they name hurricanes after women." (That man should be denied sex for a really long time.)

For two years my husband has been badgering me: "When are you going to write it?" For two years I've resisted. But he persisted: "When are you going to write about every man's journey?" Every *man's* journey?

But the time has come. Finally, in deference to the man I vowed to torment—I mean, love—for eternity, I'm going to write about what a bitch I am at a certain time of the month.

At some point, each and every month, my husband looks at me and in a V-8 moment says, very loudly, "*Ooooh!*" This is every month for 23 years of marriage. And each time it's as if it never happened before. Either my husband is a glutton for punishment, or he has a very bad memory. Yogi Berra, he says, must have been talking about his wife when he said, "It's like déjà vu all over again."

Of course, each time as he slaps his forehead, I want to reach over and slap him silly. My husband says you shouldn't be the Sherman male standing nearest to me during that time of the month. If you are, get out of the way. But that's not really fair; I would slap *anybody* standing close to me who feels the need to point out what a bitch I am and what an innocent victim they are.

I keep asking my husband, "What is wrong with being a bitch?" I really believe my edge, especially my hormonal edge, makes me extremely effective. When I have to deal with customer service people, I usually make the call in the 25th day of my cycle. I get what I want every time. I find my best cleaning tantrums occur at that time too—usually, because I've taken some child's drawer in fury and dumped it on the ground. When else are you going to get so organized?

I'm not just mean—I'm also emotional. Recently, we were 20 minutes late for a dinner with dear friends. I screamed like a madwoman at my husband for being late. Honestly, even *I* couldn't figure out why I was so upset about 20 minutes. When we got to dinner and our friends were fine with our tardiness, I started crying about how lucky we were to have such good friends. My husband couldn't understand the sentimental turnaround. My friend, who works out with me and who therefore knows my schedule intimately, looked at the two of us and said, "Don't you know she's due?" *Oooooh.*

Between the cathartic crying and the maniacal screaming, I'm exhausted. Also, I'm really old and have served my reproductive purpose, so I shouldn't have to be going through this any more. I am an anomaly of evolution. In medieval times I would have been dead at 14, not going through this at 45. Now we live so long we have to manage a reproductive system that is working well beyond its need. As a result, there is the miracle of 60-year-olds having babies. But there is also the consequence of a lot of traumatized husbands. There's a reason my husband loves our little dog, Curley, so much. He says, "It's because she's been spayed."

Of course, my views on this subject were formed early on when I first "became a woman." You see, the gynecologist my mother sent me to talk to happened to be my father. My female role model came from a brochure in Daddy's office. It was weird enough, as a young girl reaching adolescence, to have a father who was a gynecologist. Schoolmates would taunt me with, "Your father is a lady doctor."

It got so bad, I made up an explanation for his choice of specialty. I would tell people that one day, on a dark and windy night, a famous gynecologist came to my father's house and saved my grandmother on the kitchen table, and my father vowed that he, too, would become a gynecologist. I told the story so many times, I started to believe it.

Eventually, it got back to my father from one of his patients. He came home and explained the totally logical explanation for his line of work: He wanted a specialty, he wanted to be a surgeon and he wanted to be connected to the whole family. I liked my fairy tale story much more. And I was still embarrassed. So my father reassured me with these exact words: "Pamela, they all look alike except for your mother."

My situation was made even more mystifying by the fact that my mother was a Freudian psychoanalyst. So my parental advice was very confusing. Every time I had a headache, my father would tell me to take two aspirins and my mother would ask me who was I mad at.

My older sister tried to help me by telling me I had just received THE CURSE. How comforting. But this is supposed to be a beautiful time for woman. For those of us who read *The Red Tent*, we know that, historically, we're supposed to move into a beautiful fruit-laden tent and take care of each other. Now I realize there was another reason for that tent. The husbands wanted their wives just to disappear.

Every time my husband points out how hard I am to live with, I tell him that because of this particular bodily function, I gave him his beautiful children and he should shut up and be grateful. But now my offspring are starting to notice the monthly rants. My son is beginning to really understand the concept, "When Mommy no happy, ain't nobody happy." He has taken to speaking to me as if I were insane—which only makes me more insane. (Of course he's going to read this column, which will bring together all of his sex-education classes into one easy lesson.)

I asked my friends if their children notice the change in their mother's personality. One friend was sitting with her son while they observed a woman having a tantrum in a store. He looked at her and said, "You act like that woman, Mom, but only once a month." My nephews learned early on, "Don't make eye contact."

But is it any wonder I'm so exasperated? I have basically one good week a month. I call it my skinny week. I have tried every which way to manage the problem. Hormonal drugs, which just made me fat and even bitchier. Hormonal drugs with anti-depressants, which just made me depressed. And now I'm on to acupuncture and holistic nutrition. I take all sorts of vitamins and herbs and I have changed my diet. And I am totally mellow—*while on the acupuncture table*. It's when

I leave and go home and scream at my family that I wonder if it's really working.

I hear there are new breakthroughs. I have one friend who is taking a little pill so she only gets it every three months. My fear is every three months my family would have to hide the knives.

Recently my doctor laughed at me when I outlined my list of ailments (she was pregnant at the time and can be excused her cynicism). She told me I was a typical miserable woman of my age. How comforting. She said her happiest group of patients are all those women in their 50s who have gone through menopause (which explains the popularity of that show *Menopause The Musical;* everyone in the audience has either been through it or is looking forward to it).

But when I go through it, I'll no longer have an excuse for my behavior: screaming at the telephone company, crying at ads on television and cleaning furiously. I'll be like my husband, who can be bitchy and emotional many a time but has no excuse for his behavior. There is no V-8 moment on my part. Just endless exasperation.

That's okay. I'll get him back. He thinks it's going to get better when I go through menopause. Doesn't he realize that he has a 9-year-old daughter who is coming up in the ranks to torture him? You go, girl.

16

Separate Vacations Together

MAY/JUNE 2008

My husband and I met while living abroad, and traveling became an important part of our relationship. For years we went without a couch because we spent all of our disposable income on travel. We would go anywhere and stay anywhere.

Our first weekend get-away while living in London was to a tacky hotel jammed with Labor Party conventioneers in Brighton, England. Because we had no money, we visited the great European capitals staying in cold hostels or B&Bs, eating take-out under electric blankets while dropping money into coin-operated heating systems. For ease of travel, I carried a backpack and no hair dryer.

Things have changed for us over the years. Now I'm known for traveling with too many valises. Whatever happened to those days when civilized people traveled with a steamer trunk filled with an outfit for every day? They've been lost to the 50-pound weight limit—with 10 of those pounds taken up by luggage wheels. I'm balanced out by my husband, who's known for wearing the same T-shirt (usually from a college he didn't attend) for most of our vacation, until it walks home by itself.

I have hotel standards now, too. It doesn't have to be fancy, but heat is required. And don't put me near an ice machine. Okay, I'll admit, I'm picky. I'm constantly changing rooms because they aren't quite perfect. My husband was once so frustrated about this, he finally said to a front-desk clerk upon arrival, "Why don't you just give her the second room first and then we'll all be happy."

At the same time, I'm appreciative like Julia Roberts in *Pretty Woman*. When I get upgraded to a suite, I dance around it with glee. I love free shower caps, toothbrushes and mouthwash. Slippers and a terry-cloth robe send me into ecstasy.

Over the years, my husband and I have come to realize we have different interests when we travel. My husband likes to soak up the local scene. Walk the streets. Hang out in coffee bars and restaurants. Even go grocery-shopping to see what the locals like to eat.

I like to cross all the top-10 tourist attractions off my list, including every museum, stately home and double-decker bus tour. I'm a sucker for a $20 guide book or a guide with an umbrella teaching me irrelevant facts about plumbing in the 15th century.

And then there are the do-nothing vacations where I cannot possibly do-nothing. I might bring 10 books with the fantasy I will just sit staring at the water. But after about 10 minutes, I'll be looking at the Daily Activities sheet, begging my husband to do Tae Bo on the beach.

After 11 years of marriage we finally reached a compromise on how to travel together. He would sit in a square and drink coffee while I toured the church crypts below. He would sit at a café and watch the locals while I shopped in the surrounding streets. And in the ultimate compromise of the willing husband, he even let me pack some of my clothes in his suitcase.

We successfully negotiated through years of family trips, business trips, relaxing trips, even sight-seeing trips (like the time my husband walked into the Louvre and immediately walked out, just so he could now say he'd been there).

And then we had kids.

Someone once told me that once you have children, you don't go on vacation; you just change the scenery. Because when you travel with your kids, you have to replicate life at home. When they're babies, you have to fit cribs, bouncy seats, and diapers into luggage that used to hold what you once thought were essentials—you know, *clothes*. When they grow up you have to bring all the electronic items and accompanying chargers so that they won't be bored as you travel to your destination. Suddenly any hotel room with a room-darkening shade and room for a crib will do.

Upon getting pregnant, I lamented that we would never travel again. I was wrong. The wanderlust was in our blood, so by the time my son was 3, he had his passport stamped three times. When he was 5 months old, we took him to Spain for a friend's wedding. My valises were packed with 60 jars of baby food and two weeks' worth of diapers. I exceeded the weight limit, and I still ran short of supplies eventually. Try buying diapers when you can't read Spanish. Who knew that "Grandiosos" were adult diapers? (Which reminds me of trying to buy contraceptives for my husband in Paris once.

"Petite ou grand?" they asked me at the pharmacy. I looked at my husband and said "Medium" with a French accent. They burst out laughing and put a small box and a large box on the counter. They were referring to the size of the box. Ooooh.).

And Jerusalem wasn't easy with a 2-year-old. Holy sites aren't easy to get to as it is. I was five-and-a-half-months pregnant with our second child, it was 120 degrees—and 2000 years ago there were no such things as ramps for strollers.

Still, after my daughter was born, we kept traveling. On a trip to California, the stewardess chucked my son under the chin, then looked at the baby and said, "How cute. Is this your baby sister's first trip on a plane?" My son replied, "Are you kidding? She's been to California 'shree' times." She was 4 months old.

We've done the required trips to Disneyland and Disney World. We've paid $150 for admission to zoos and aquariums that look the same the world over. We traversed the same kind of playgrounds and Starbucks we have at home and ate $25 hamburgers because there was nothing else to eat. The gift shop souvenirs we bought sit in the kids' drawers and could have financed an entire trip to Europe.

For the most part, my children don't remember these trips. So why bother leaving home? Well, for one, I have to believe that the ease with which they travel now and the awe that they have visiting new places started early, from those trips. But mostly, it's when we're away from our everyday existence that our family remembers how much we enjoy being together. I'm amazed how my kids, who never really even talk to each other (or who fight when they do), make forts in the back of the car during long rides, hiding underneath blankets and whispering fiercely.

For fear that we would lose "family bonding-time," my husband insists that we not travel with friends. Also, we like our friends too much to travel with them. But sometimes you can't avoid seeing people you know. We have one friend who was traveling to Miami at the same time. She innocently said, "Why don't we get together?" I had to explain that my curmudgeon (I mean my husband) really likes to get away from everything and everyone on vacation. Every time we saw her on the beach she would hide behind me or pretend not to see him.

Finally our kids are at an age where they will have lasting impressions of our family trips. Last year when they were 10 and 8, we took them to London. I listed 150 places we *had* to see. They loved every one of them. By the last day, it was my husband who was exhausted. For the sake of family harmony, we agreed to part ways for that last day. I took our daughter to St. Paul's Cathedral and the Tate Modern Gallery. He took our son on a "Daddy adventure." When we met for tea, our daughter went on and on about drawing in the galleries and the beautiful Cathedral. My son said, "We had the best time, Mom. We hung out in Chinatown and got chair massages."

We've just returned from a trip as far away as you can go without going to Antarctica—Australia. I was so anxious about the impending 18 hours of flying, I asked my doctor for a prescription for Xanax. I had that Xanax in my pocket the entire flight but I never took it because I realized that traveling with my family has taught me that I can get through almost anything.

My daughter, who can't sit still for a 10-minute car ride, peacefully slept for most of the flight. After we arrived, my husband graciously put up with bus tours filled with Japanese tourists, who almost pushed us into a crocodile pit with their cameras. I even agreed to search out Sydney's Chinatown for the best dim sum for my son. It was my daughter who insisted that her father take her to a contemporary art museum and a chair massage. And I did the most intrepid things I've ever done on vacation. I swam with huge manta rays in the Great Barrier Reef, and I climbed the Sydney Harbour Bridge in the pouring rain with my son (earning cool-mom points for years).

My husband said that moments on this trip count as some of the top 10 best in his life—right up there with meeting me and the day I gave birth to our children. Upon our return, my son and daughter yelled "Good night!" between the walls of their rooms. My son even called out to my daughter, "Hey, let's meet in our dreams." That's worth the price of admission anywhere.

17

• • • • • • •

What's in a Name? A Lot.

JULY/AUGUST 2008

When my son was *in utero*, everyone kept asking us what we were going to call him. We told them him Tecumsah, as in William Tecumsah Sherman. This drove my parents crazy. "You are not going to name our grandson Tecumsah. What are you thinking?" We weren't serious, but I felt we needed some element of surprise since we already knew so much about him, like his gender.

I also felt I needed to meet my son before we named him. I thought his name would reveal itself at birth. This sounds crazy, given what children look like at the moment of birth, all squishy and amoeba-like. Babies look like babies, not Harrys, Davids, or Sams.

But when he finally arrived on a rainy St. Patrick's Day, as soon as we looked at him we knew his name was Zach. We just knew.

Two years later, when we found out we were having a girl this time, we argued about her potential names. I wanted to name her Bette, after Bette Midler. My husband, who hates the Divine Miss M, refused. He suggested Liza, which reminded me too much of Liza Minelli (look how she turned out). We liked Zoe, but then our children would have sounded like a bad vaudeville team. I imagined them singing, "We're Zachy and Zoe and we're bursting with love."

So then I thought of the name Phoebe, after my favorite character in Shakespeare's *As You Like It.* But another couple we knew had a Zach and they named their daughter Phoebe six months before our daughter was born. We were worried it would be confusing and we would look like we were copying them. (Now we don't even live near them.)

Finally we narrowed it down to Talia, Olivia and Eliza and waited to meet her. As it turned out, she just didn't look like a Talia at birth (and the more I thought about it, the name Talia reminded me of a bronzed machine-gun-wielding Israeli soldier).

Olivia was eliminated quickly when the labor nurse told me that there had been 12 Olivias in the prior two weeks. I didn't want her to meet herself coming and going. Silly me, I never considered that she might never have met those other 12 Olivias.

One baby book described the personality of Eliza as a plucky English whore. I like plucky, at least. And she was an Eliza from the moment she arrived. She was totally pink, like the pink roses from the opening credits of *My Fair Lady*, the story of Eliza Doolittle, plucky English flower girl. I figured she'd have a lifetime of people singing "Wouldn't It Be Loverly" to her. But no one gets it. She's 9 now, and even her paternal grandfather can't get her name right. He calls her Elijah. His birthday checks somehow get deposited into her account, anyway, so we don't have the heart to correct him.

We were lucky because the names we chose caused no family arguments. I know people who are still angry that their siblings "stole" their baby names. Or women angry at their husbands for usurping the naming of their infant while the wives were drugged and incoherent. One friend begged that their daughter not be given a certain name she hated. She woke up from her twilight sleep and realized that, in her delirium, she had happily agreed to the name.

And then there are the nicknames that can take over your real name. I found it very amusing that after our daughter was born, people kept asking us, "What do you call her for short?" Isn't her name short enough? My sister should have officially named her son "Matthew-Not-Matt" because that's how she introduced him for his first five years. Then she gave up. He's Matt now.

My husband is from Geneva, N.Y., where no one uses real names. They have nicknames like Stinky and Booger (all descriptive). This was very confusing—I could never keep all of his friends straight. Once when we were first married he told me that a childhood friend of his, Mike, was going to come to our apartment for dinner. During dinner, my husband and Mike talked about their old friends, Sack, Dinky, Buzzy, Chico and Pugsley. At one point I asked, "What happened to your friend Fonzi?" They both laughed. Mike was Fonzi.

My son has carried on the nickname tradition among his lacrosse buddies. One friend is called Mac. My husband asked if Mac was his given name and the dad said, "I named him a classic Scottish name and after my favorite scotch, MacAllan's." When my son heard this, he said to my husband, "Thank goodness you didn't name me Absolut Citron."

Rather than reduce your name to a diminutive, you can always decide your name just doesn't fit you. One friend told me her friend Shirley has decided to rename herself Lily. This won't be easy for her friends and family, of course, who have called her Shirley all her life. But inside, she has always felt she was a Lily, and she is finally going to be that Lily.

Maybe all those children with ridiculous celebrity names like Brooklyn, Apple, Dweezil and B9 (whose parents apparently love bingo) are going to grow up and change their names to Fred, Sue and Bob.

We knew one woman who, about to change her marital status, changed her last name *and* her first name. She felt she just wasn't meant to be a Sue married to Lou. After the separation, my husband saw the dejected husband, who explained that his wife had come home one day and started calling herself Katrina Pilar. And Katrina Pilar was someone who wanted to be on her own.

That may sound extreme, but trying on new names is irresistible. Who hasn't played the game where you pick out the name of your first dog and the first street you lived on to arrive at your drag queen or stripper name? Mine is Charlie Thomas. My husband would be Jocko Lochland.

And then there are the people whose names seemed to have determined their inevitable professions. Like the gynecologist, Dr. Hymen. Or the famous Rochester urologist who has performed many a vasectomy, Dr. Stop.

My father loved the name Pamela. But each time my parents had a baby, my mother kept overruling him. Finally, she gave him a turn with me, their fourth. I realize now that it was just the luck of birth order that gave me my name. There was no magical moment when he looked at me and said, "Ah, that's a Pamela."

That might explain something, because I'm *so* not a Pamela, which means "honeyed sweetness". Growing up, I felt my name didn't fit me at all. I was destined for the stage, and I thought it would never be a great stage name. Would *you* pay to see Pamela Weinstein as Lady MacBeth? When I was a kid I used to come up with pretend stage names. It could be I fell in love with my husband's last name, Sherman, as much as I fell in love with him, because it totally worked as my stage name.

And far worse than Pamela (which was usually reserved for when I was in trouble), my family liked to call me Pammy. People who don't know me call me Pammy innocently, thinking it's endearing. I do not like to be called Pammy. It's overly-familiar and makes me feel like I'm 8. It bugs me so much, I always say to those unsuspecting few—in as honey-sweet a voice as I can without seeming psychotic—"*Don't EVER call me by that name.*"

But over time, I feel I've come to define my name, not the other way around. This became clear to me when I was admitted to the Virginia Bar, and I finally embraced all my names.

In Virginia, the pomp and circumstance includes a ceremony in front of the entire Supreme Court of the Commonwealth (Talk about name issues: Virginia isn't even called a state). The chief justice then calls the name and school of each new member of the bar, and each member stands to acknowledge the chief.

The chief called the names in a syrupy drawl: "Beauregard Beaufort the Third from the great college of William and Mary, Ashley Wilkes the Fourth from University of Virginia founded by Thomas Jefferson, Scarlett O'Hara from Cherry Blossom Law School." After an interminable amount of time, he finally called my name, very tentatively: "Pamela Lisa Weinstein Sherman from the Benjamin N. Cardozo School of Law of Yeshiva University?" I proudly stood up, waved at the chief justice and said in my best New Yawk accent, "Dat's me."

Today, you can call me Pam, Pamela, Sherm, Mom, Suburban Outlaw, Charlie Thomas, or even a four-letter word if needed (I sometimes do). But please, and I'll say this nicely, don't, ever, call, me, Pammy.

18

School's In, Forever

SEPTEMBER/OCTOBER 2008

I was a very dedicated student. My husband describes me as "the girl in the front of the class." The one who always has just one more question. The one who asks about the homework assignment on a Friday afternoon. You know, the annoying one.

He says he married me because his grades were too low during our semester abroad. Sitting in the back of the classroom, he picked me to be his girlfriend when he learned I was getting straight A's. He figured if I got him through the semester, he would be eternally grateful and prove it by marrying me (and I always thought he loved me for my body).

I liked school so much, I even taught undergraduates once as an adjunct professor at my alma mater. Of course, they sat there with their arms crossed, waiting for me to entertain them. I tried my hardest, like a desperate performer during a bad vaudeville act. That's when I realized then I preferred being a student.

Even after I left school, I loved to take classes. Cooking, pilates, speed-reading. The nice thing about being an adult student is that it's easier to have an attitude; no principals are involved. Still, even though it didn't matter anymore, I was still grade-conscious. I was mortified when I took a Thai cooking class with a friend who had trained at the Cordon Bleu in Paris and the teacher told us to throw away our Pad Thai because it was so bad. My friend vowed never to take another class with me because I distracted her by asking too many questions (maybe it was all that wine we drank during the class).

Naturally, when I decided to become an actor after seven years of practicing law, I figured the first thing I had to do was...take a class. I studied Shakespeare and singing (my teacher told me I was the bravest actor who couldn't sing). I even studied something called Alexander Technique, where my teacher "gave birth" to me.

I took scene-study classes late at night in really bad parts of Washington, D.C., with teachers who made us stare at the wall just to see if "something would happen." Something did happen: I got bored out of my mind.

And talk about not fitting in. There I was a 30-something lawyer taking classes after work with my pantyhose still on, among 20-something actors all wearing black and smoking cigarettes. I loved it.

After my law firm went out of business, I took it as a sign that I should return to school full-time. I studied acting in New York at The Neighborhood Playhouse, famous for graduating Dustin Hoffman and Robert Duvall. There, we were instructed to stare at another actor (an improvement over the wall) and repeat over and over, "I like your shirt," until "something would happen." Something did happen: I got really pissed off.

So then I flew off to Oxford, England, to study more Shakespeare. Suffering for my art, I lived in a 13th-century dorm room with no air-conditioning and no hot water. We ate in a dining room *a la* Hogwarts, but the food wasn't as magical. Because I was one of the few "more mature" students, I had to sneak my husband in past the security guards when he visited me in my dorm room.

There, I learned about stage combat: I was thrown around the quad by a dangerous young actor performing Jacobean tragedy. The bruises were proof I was working hard, and I told my husband I wanted to keep studying. As he squirmed in my twin dorm-room bed, he pleaded, "Why don't you try just acting for a while?" So I did, until the next life milestone came: parenthood.

Time to study again. While pregnant, I took two birthing classes: one at the hospital, where I learned about which drugs to take during childbirth. The other on the floor of someone's home, where I learned drugs were bad—all I really needed was a birthing plan.

There was the breastfeeding class taught by Mary Lou Teets (for real). And yoga for pregnancy taught by a woman named Geeny Feeny. She made our husbands come with us so we could give birth to *them* by lying down and "pushing them out" between our legs. Geeny was also the woman who, when I ended up having a C-section after 36 hours of labor, told me I had "failed the course" because I didn't visualize dilation effectively.

So after that, I was eager to raise my GPA. I took a course about handling an infant: washing, feeding and getting them to sleep. I received many hand-outs, which I dutifully placed into notebooks. Of course, they were meaningless once the baby arrived. When my son was born I forgot everything I learned, especially swaddling. Poor kid was very cold for the first two months.

I took my first discipline class when my son was 4-months-old. This class taught that if your child is banging on a glass table with a toy, you say, "If you keep banging on the glass with that toy, I'll take away the toy." Instead of screaming, *"STOP BANGING THAT TOY!"*

When my kids started elementary school, I graduated to the "Parenting with Love and Logic" class. We were taught that, starting at an early age, if our kids didn't want to wear a coat we should let them go out and be cold; then they would learn the logical consequence of not wearing a coat. But I discovered the logical consequence of loving them with logic is pneumonia because they went out without a coat. Or worse, the school calls you out because you let your 5-year-old make a decision.

I did find my new parenting guru through a class called "1, 2, 3 Magic." In this class I learned that parents make two huge mistakes: We talk too much and we get too emotional. That makes my husband and me the perfect storm of parenting: He talks too much and I get too emotional.

The teacher told us that we are supposed to say "one… two…three…" to diffuse a discipline problem. If, by the time you have counted three, your children haven't towed the line, you put them in a time-out for as many minutes as their age. Thank goodness I didn't wait until my son was 16 to try this.

For an overachiever, these parenting classes can be very disheartening—mostly because the real-life execution usually has nothing to do with the theoretical. I must have failed this class, too, because I keep forgetting to count "one, two, three."

Or, when I do remember, I'm screaming by the time I get to three.

Okay, so I'm not the A student I used to be. But at least I'm trying. My husband refuses to attend classes and therefore can never keep up with the program. I leave the reading material in the bathroom for him, but he chooses to read almost anything before he reads the parenting books—he'll even read the packaging on my feminine products before those books.

One friend told me she went through her entire education trying to skip classes. Why, now that she is a grown-up, would she choose to take more classes? She even cut her knitting classes when she decided to take that up in her 40s. She thinks I'm nuts: "Your babies were coming out even if you never took the childbirth class, and your children are going to grow up whether you take a parenting class or not."

While that may be true, all my classes make me feel some control in situations where I don't have enough—childbirth, a new career, even cooking. And I get the validation of a teacher telling me if I'm doing well or if I need to throw out the food I just made. I'm not sure what class I'll take next. If there is a class for groping your way through life, I'll take it and sit right up front.

It's not often in post-graduation life that you get to return to the simple world of the grading system. As an actor, I'd give myself an A for bravery. As a parent, so far I'd give myself an A+ for effort (who knows how they'll eventually turn out). But no matter how much I study the recipe, my Pad Thai still gets an F.

19

• • • • • • •

Bulk Fashion?
A Shopoholic Confesses.

November/December 2008

When I appeared in *Shear Madness* on stage in Washington, D.C., my character was asked where she'd spent the day. "Shopping, shopping, shopping" was my opening line. Never in my entire theater career had I intoned a line I could relate to more. I nailed it every performance, sometimes 10 shows a week, for a year and a half. I had no need to explore my character's motivation to express that line. It was—and has been—my truth for a very long time.

The night before my wedding, my father ceremoniously asked me for the "emergency" American Express card he had given me while I was studying abroad. "Emergency" had never been specifically defined, and I had broadened the definition over time to include items such as those totally cute Frye boots I just had to have. On the eve of my nuptials, my father proceeded to cut that card into shreds, laughing maniacally while muttering to himself, "She's not my problem anymore." Yes, I was still excited about the future with my betrothed, but the credit card shards also left me terrified about the future with the other great love of my life, shopping.

And really, who is to blame for my illicit love affair? My parents, of course. My mother taught me to buy in bulk at a very early age. Bulk fashion buying, that is. Before outlet malls existed, she would take my sister and me to discount stores—places deep in the heart of Brooklyn and New Jersey that sold discounted designer-wear with the labels ripped out. We shopped with abandon. The dressing rooms were communal, and there was no time to be shy. It was discount, after all. And we weren't paying for it. We would sneak the bags into the house later. If my dad was in a good mood, we would do a fashion show for him.

Really, the discounts couldn't have mattered much because we made up for them in volume. My mother would pay lip service to narrowing down our purchases at the cash register. But for the most part, if it fit, we bought it. When I became a lawyer and bought my first suit from Lord & Taylor, my mother wept. "Didn't I teach you better than to buy retail?!"

My father was just as bad. When he passed away. I saw the extent of his shopping fever. How many men can boast a closet the same size as their wives? How many men own five leather jackets—one of them in orange leather? My dad had more golf shirts with their tags still on than you would find in an actual golf shop. Bagging up his clothes for donation, I realized I had to end my days of bulk shopping or else my children would one day be bagging up my ponchos, dusters, and leggings with the same head-shaking disdain.

So I'm trying to tell myself that clothing is not toilet paper and should not be purchased in bulk. I have one friend with a very small closet. As a result she agonizes over what she should bring into it. "I have to consider every piece of clothing and whether it deserves to have a home in my tiny little closet," she says.

Whereas I've always had more of an open-door policy. When we first moved into our house in Bethesda, I felt like Natalie Wood in *Miracle on 34th Street*, who knew the house at the end of the movie was hers because Kris Kringle had left his cane by the fireplace. I knew I was home in the house as soon as I saw the closet. The enormous closet with the shoe rack that fit more than 100 pairs was meant to be mine. When we moved out of that house, one of my friends called me and asked if she could come over to say goodbye...to my closet.

Now I'm forced to share a closet with my husband. This is terrible because whenever I bring something new into the closet, my husband instinctively knows it's there. He has some sort of new-clothes radar. I have to shred the evidence as soon as I pull in the driveway. My husband never tells me I look great in an outfit. Instead he says, "Is that new?" Nope. I got it...a week ago.

Theoretically, this should help me kick my addiction. But I'm a slave to fashion. If the magazines tell me to buy ribbed leggings, I'm out there buying ribbed leggings.

Each year I give bags and bags of clothes to charity, but it doesn't seem to make a dent. Perhaps if I only buy what I need instead of what I want, this could lead to a cure. Do I really need another pair of black shoes? (Well, if they're patent leather, probably yes.) My concept of need and my husband's concept of need have always been different. He doesn't think he needs new pants, even as his frayed cuffs dwindle down to nothing. I need new pants because the magazines tell me that wide leg is in. He doesn't think the T-shirt from 1987 should be given away—to him, it's finally comfortable. I think the

T-shirt I wore last summer should go to Goodwill because yellow is so out.

In reality, I don't *love* to shop. I don't meet up with friends and tool around the mall. When I shop, I'm on a mission. It's about going in for the kill: bagging that bargain or that hot item of the season. It's like big-game hunting, only instead of elephants I'm hunting shoes.

When we first moved to Rochester, I lamented the loss of Nordstrom and my favorite Bethesda boutiques. Yet my husband tells me I've done great things for the Rochester economy as I've come to appreciate all the retail that Rochester has to offer. One friend, who was visiting when we first moved here, squealed with delight because she found her favorite T-shirt in an adorable boutique in Pittsford. She looked at me and said, "You're going to be fine here."

I'm really trying to get better. I've always liked to visit my favorite department stores when traveling, but now I'm trying to think of them as fashion museums. I walk through Barney's and Bergdorf's the way other people walk through the Metropolitan Museum of Art. And really, with the price of a hand bag in these stores, I might as well be making an offer on a Rembrandt. Who is buying this stuff? My 9-year-old has learned this concept and asks me, "Mom, can we go shop in the windows?"

And, while I'm confessing, it's not just clothes that feed my addiction. I can point to almost every item in my house and tell you if it came from T.J. Maxx, Marshall's or Bed Bath and Beyond *and* how much I paid for it. It's like fashion for my house.

They say the first step on the road to recovery is admitting you have a problem. And I've changed. Really. I've decided to shop in my own closet for a while. Goodness knows there's enough in there. A few weeks back, I took my credit cards out of my wallet (I kept the scissors in the drawer, though, so no promises…).

I've also tried some substitutes. I read somewhere that lipstick is recession-proof because even if you can't buy a new dress, you can always buy a $6 lipstick. So I'm learning to wear lipstick.

My husband cried tears of joy when he read a draft of this article; his interventions have never worked before. But like any reformed addict, I can't say when a relapse is coming. For now, when I feel the urge to buy something, I'll just go to Wegmans. It's safe in there…isn't it?

20

• • • • • • •

Happy New Year, You're Perfect, Now Change

December 31 is a day filled with expectations and disappointment. Every year I hope that my New Year's Eve will be special and exciting. I imagine black tie and fireworks. Usually I get sick kids and a husband sleeping on the couch.

Beyond the failed expectations of the party, there's the added pressure of my list of New Year's resolutions. Not the list for the upcoming year, but last year's list. Every year, as we plan to celebrate the incoming New Year, I'm reminded that I have completely failed my annual to-do list. I end my year feeling really bad.

Until last year. Last year I made a change. I decided to make resolutions for other people. This was so much easier than making them for myself. I could tell people what I knew was best for them and feel really good that I was helping other people.

I started with my husband. I hate how he wears sweatpants all the time, so I decided a good resolution for him was to wear real pants. Another resolution for him wasn't to lose weight but to stop *saying* he's going to lose weight. Last year, I decided he just needed to show restraint (a goal I set for myself, as well). He lost 20 pounds. I also would like him to stop barbecuing so much—the meat ends up really charred and hard to eat. He didn't listen to that one.

As for my kids, here's a great New Year's resolution: Grow up. Now that's not too hard, is it? It's going to happen anyway. And they'll feel good about themselves.

I wasn't completely one-sided. I let them make resolutions for me, too. I love being told what to do. If someone tells me to do something, I'm actually more likely to do it because I am really good at following directions. It's probably why I became a lawyer (all those rules) and then became an actor (you have someone called a director telling you what to do).

Here are their resolutions for me. My husband wanted me to stop telling him what to do (that was a problem, since I'd just given him a list of what to do). My daughter wanted me to yell less. My son wanted me to learn to play Guitar Hero.

These resolutions were so much easier to follow than the resolutions I used to make before I had children. I used to force my husband to fill out a blank greeting card with our very complicated resolutions before we started our revels for the night. Recently, I found the cards from 1993 to 1998 (all the others have gone missing).

The resolutions were reflective of our marriage at the time: Don't control. Don't over-analyze. Don't be insensitive or overly sensitive. Where were the normal ones, like "eat less"? Well, this was before we had kids. We had plenty of time to contemplate our navels and that of our partner.

Sometime in 1994 we got a dog. The resolution followed: Care for another living being. Good thing we didn't have kids at the time; we actually needed a resolution to tell us to *care for another living being.* Should we need a resolution? My favorite resolution was from 1995: "Helping Harpo to become a mature dog with love and time."

If your family won't make resolutions for you, your government will. Here's a list of the most popular New Year's resolutions, which I found on the U.S. government Website, www.usa.gov.

1. Lose 10 pounds.
2. Get out of debt/save money.
3. Spend time with family.
4. Do for others.
5. Quit smoking/drinking.
6. Get a better job.
7. Get fit.
8. Help others.
9. Get organized.
10. Reduce stress.

Why does the U.S. government keep track of—or even care—what our New Year's resolutions will be? Especially since the U.S. government doesn't exactly succeed at these resolutions itself. Get out of debt?? And where are the obvious government-issued resolutions, like "Pack an emergency kit."

Another Website—www.goalsguys.com—run by a self-help guru who calls himself the Goalsguy, aims to establish a New Year's Resolution Week (because that's how long they'll last, I suppose). In fact, all the self-help books that we never get around to reading are really just telling us to stick to our New Year's resolutions. It's a huge industry and we help these gurus fulfill their No. 1 resolution: Make lots of money (new New Year's resolution: Write self-help book).

I actually believe in the power of visualization and affirmations, but with bite-size goals. Perhaps what is daunting is trying to maintain resolutions for a whole year. Studies have shown that only 12 percent of us actually keep our New Year's resolutions beyond three months (thus the huge spike in fitness club memberships from January to March). What if we were all honest and said, "*This month* I resolve to..."? Or why promise at all? Just say you'll *try* to ... (fill in the blank).

New Year's resolutions, it turns out, have existed since early Rome. Janus, the king with two faces who looked backward on the past and forward to the future, was the symbol of the start of the new year. Romans would ask their enemies for forgiveness and then exchange gifts. It's hard to imagine an ancient Roman making a resolution to lose weight. I'd like to think they were thinking about more important things, like keeping their empire from crumbling.

A lot of people have elaborate rituals surrounding the resolutions they end up not keeping. My sister-in-law has a black-tie New Year's Eve party, and she makes everyone come prepared with a New Year's resolution, which she seals up in an envelope and opens the next year. The next year, assuming she can find the envelope, they open it and see which ones they kept. What a bummer of a party.

But my sister-in-law is a University of Chicago MBA and very organized. She makes elaborate charts of her own resolutions by category: charity, personal growth, major projects. That way, whatever she does within that category makes her feel successful, even if it's a little thing. An MBA put to good use.

Another friend phones a childhood friend a few days after Christmas to write out their resolutions. She puts the list in her wallet and carries it with her all year so she can cross the item off the list as she does it. She says she feels better about herself just by crossing something off the page (like a shopping list of personal improvement).

One friend loves that she gets to make New Year's resolutions twice, for the Jewish New Year and for the regular New Year. Oy, two lists. Every year her resolutions include "read *Moby Dick*." She still hasn't read it, but it looks good on her nightstand.

One woman told me she has had the same resolution for years: Drink more water. She says she is always successful. I told her this is not a good resolution because if she keeps improving, some year she'll drink too much and float away.

One friend from Poland who is married to a Brazilian asked me, "What is a New Year's resolution?" Apparently their governments don't have a list.

My favorite is my party-girl friend. Her resolutions include take more trips, go out to lunch more and have more fun. She never fails.

And then there is my do-good friend. She resolves each year to do something for someone else. One year she put her church donation on automatic withdrawal. Did *she* meet her obligation or did the electronic banking system? This past year she resolved to give more blood. She told me every time you give blood you lose a pound, thus killing two resolutions with one stone.

This year I'm aiming for success. So here goes:

1. Breathe.
2. Pet dog.
3. Do laundry.
4. Pay bills.
5. Yell.
6. Eat.
7. Watch T.V.
8. Shower.
9. Shop for food.
10. Love my family.

I know that last one is a mushy one, but it beats having to pack an emergency kit. I know I'd never bother.

21

. . . .

The Techno-Cowboy
Stole My Heart

MARCH/APRIL 2009

When Carrie Bradshaw in *Sex and the City* found a man with all the right moves, she decided it was time to "take a luvah." Now, I've done the same.

Mine is my computer guy, and it's not even a secret. His wife schedules our meetings, and my husband approves. In fact, I think my husband has his own secret crush on him, too.

Shane is his name, and just like Shane from the western, he's the strong, silent type. He even looks a little like Alan Ladd. Shane services a need in our family that benefits us all. He prevents *me*, not just my computer, from melting down.

As my techno-luvah, he doesn't even need to be here to satisfy. Shane installed a little icon on our computer that moves the mouse remotely. This is so much better than cyber-sex because at the end, your broken computer is fixed and you didn't have to do a thing.

I know that I live in an age of technological wonder. I should be grateful for the benefits of the Internet, the power of gigabytes, the instant gratification of running hot water. I certainly take advantage of technology. I'm no Luddite. I do not type my columns on a typewriter or dial a rotary phone.

But I'm definitely missing the technology gene. I always fall short in understanding how the darn things work or, more importantly, why they fail. And when technology fails me, *I* break down. I get all sweaty and freak out, yelling at everyone who happens to be close by. I bang on my computer, thinking that will help.

Apparently it's a condition. There are all sorts of studies out there about people with techno-phobia. I am not unique. Unlike children who grow up technologically facile, I am what they've labeled a "technological immigrant" (is there a virtual Ellis Island out there somewhere?).

I always tell my kids that more has happened in the world technologically since their dad and I were born in the early 1960s than perhaps will happen in their lifetimes. While we haven't reached *Jetsons* territory, we're close. Who could have predicted microwaves—or microwave popcorn, for that matter? Tiny televisions and enormous flat-screen TVs? Incredible medical advances?

My parents set the stage for my techno-immigrant status. They embraced the consumer technological revolution with abandon, but always the wrong mode and always purchased too soon. Given a choice between VHS and Betamax, my poor father bought a Betamax for each television set in the house. Every family member had their own TV *with* antennas. When given the chance to buy some stock in a company called Apple, he turned it down as too cute a name. He was the first doctor with a cell phone. It was so big he had to store it in a suitcase, and when he brought it to the golf course, it practically made his golf cart list to one side.

My mother was the gadget queen in the kitchen. She never learned how to use a knife because she had a different kind of chopper for every need. The Cuisinart, for big chops; the Oscar, for medium chops; and the Mini-Cuisinart for parsley. Yes, a parsley chopper. When my mother walked into a department store the employees would fight over who would serve her. Every new technology was not only purchased for her own three kitchens (upstairs, downstairs and country) but also for her two daughters, two daughters-in-law and gift recipients of various types (weddings, engagements, even bar mitzvahs—what 13-year-old boy *doesn't* need a parsley chopper?).

I begged her to stop giving these ridiculous gadgets to me. When I finally gave away the pastry cup maker she gave me one birthday, she vowed to cross me off her list. Then again, I will be forever grateful for the apple and potato peeler she bought me. It's amazing. You put the apple on a sharp nail and stick the blade in the top of the apple, turn on the power and it peels the apple (and your finger if you're not careful) in about two seconds! God forbid you have to peel the apple yourself. You know, with your hands and a knife.

Now, even my own widowed mother has embraced computers. She even knows what a hard drive is. Of course, she still uses dial-up and her computer is almost as slow as she is. And she mostly uses it to send me chain letters and bad jokes—and to find more bad gadgets on the Internet.

Like my parents before me, we also embraced technology early on in our marriage. Our first big purchase when we were newlyweds was not a car or a house but a computer, with DOS and floppy disks. This computer was the first in a long line of computers that made me wary of technology. It ate my husband's graduate thesis, which he had worked on for months. It would take about 20 minutes to "boot up" and it was the size of a piece of furniture, taking up precious space in our tiny apartment.

We were baby-sitting my nephew one day when he put his grubby 3-year-old fingers on our keyboard. From then on, he would repeat what he learned that day from his panic-stricken Aunt Pam: " 'puters are very 'spensive—don't touch them."

How things had changed by the time we had our own children. Computer programs for 3-year-olds were a require-ment of parenthood. I *encouraged* my own darling 3-year old's grubby little hands to be all over the next incarnation of computer we owned, to give me a moment of peace.

I keep thinking my technical failings are somehow connected to my gender. (Hey, *I* can be sexist, but guys can't. Got it?). Yet many of the world's greatest technology companies are led by women, including the home-grown Xerox Corporation. Still, I've noticed how my 10-year-old daughter completely wigs out if she can't get the digital video recorder to work. Hopefully she was wigging out because I erased *The Hannah Montana Show* she desperately wanted to see, not because of some genetic failing on her part.

I'm just not sure. One friend has four children, and she insists that her three girls are technologically impaired but her son is not. By age 2, my son knew how to use Game Boys and could fix the universal remote, which completely confounds everyone else. Now, in order to level the playing field for girls, Nintendo DS is targeting young girls with pink versions and computer games that simulate fashion design and babysitting. What are next, jewel-encrusted remote controls?

But it's good they're learning young because computers are everywhere. Even my washer/dryer is a computer. Digital is a verb, noun and adjective these days. Can I say I hate digital? I miss getting my film developed and touching the paper, even if at least half my pictures were out of focus. Now my pictures are stuck in my camera, never to be seen again. Or worse. We were in Australia and my daughter's new camera wasn't working at the very moment we were seeing our first kangaroo. For some reason, she handed it to me to fix. Bad idea. To my horror, I promptly deleted 150 pictures, including the Hannah Montana concert she had gone to for her ninth birthday (maybe I just hate Hannah Montana). As I wept over her camera, *she* actually hugged *me* and said, "I forgive you, Mom."

I, however, was not so forgiving when my teenage niece and nephew decided to load a program on my computer to download music and completely crashed the "'puter," which contained the play I had written and—well, my entire life.

It was then that I met Shane.

He arrived with a briefcase and his own computer. He smelled of cigarettes. He took his shoes off and left them in the hallway without my even asking and quieted my yippy dog like a snake charmer. Then he silently got to work. He scanned. He deleted. He worked miracles. Three hours later, the virus was gone and so was my heart.

I started confessing my love to others, including my husband, who ending up stealing him away for his office. I felt like Shane had cheated on me when a friend used him to help install their new flat-screen TV and program their remotes (I didn't even know he could do that sort of thing—he's the perfect man!).

Things did get a little ugly when my husband forgot to pay his bill and Shane couldn't work for me until we paid up. But I took care of it. My kids went without their lunch money that week so I could pay him. But we were talking about fixing our local area network here! Some things take priority.

I have to say, I've missed Shane since he installed that remote device. I call him now when my computer's acting up, and I watch as my cursor moves magically across the screen. Just like Shane in that iconic movie, I know he will one day ride off into the sunset, leaving us poor homesteaders to fend for ourselves. But that's OK. I've learned a thing or two from watching him work, including the magic bullet: Turn the darn thing off.

Afterword

Now that you've read *The Suburban Outlaw: Tales from the EDGE* and understand what a Suburban Outlaw is, I hope that you are able to find the Suburban Outlaw in you and use your edge in the best possible way.

Every time you speak your mind and every time you make a difference at home and in your community, you are a Suburban Outlaw. You are a Suburban Outlaw when you start a new business or create something with your talent. You are a Suburban Outlaw when you laugh and learn about yourself. And you are a Suburban Outlaw because your dreams are part of who you are.

For those of you who still harbor secret dreams, I'll quote my one-woman show, *Pumping Josey: Life and Death in Suburbia:* "Do Something. Anything." You might have a play in you, or a novel, a quilt, or a business of some kind. And you most definitely have an edge.

In 2008, I began to take on a new edge to inspire others how to realize their dreams as I have. When a friend encouraged me to teach others how I talk to people, I realized that the concept of edge could be expanded to impact businesses. Now I use the skills I honed as an actor, writer, professor and lawyer to teach business leaders to improve their goal setting, networking, and presentation skills and be more effective communicators.

The EDGE™ training helps business leaders:

Explore:	Understand their own market
Dream:	Visualize their goals
Grow:	Out of their comfort zone
Excite:	Ignite their passion for their mission.

But that's a whole different story....

THE AUTHOR

Pam Sherman is an attorney, actress, and writer whose story has been featured in *People Magazine*. Pam has performed in theater, film, and television, including, NBC's *Homicide: Life on the Streets*, *Unsolved Mysteries*, and the long-running play, *Shear Madness* at the Kennedy Center. Her one-woman show *Pumping Josey: Life and Death*  in *Suburbia* co-written with Caleen Sinnette Jennings has played to great acclaim in many venues, including Horizons Theater.

Pam is actively involved in the international organization, Young President's Organization, Chairing the Spouse Experience for the 2009 Global Leadership Conference. Her charitable involvement has benefited many organizations including, among others, Gilda's Club of Rochester and the Randi J. Waxman Foundation. Pam has also been an Adjunct Professor at American University.

After graduating from American University and the Benjamin N. Cardozo School of Law, she practiced law in Washington, D.C. Upon leaving the law to become an actor, she attended the British American Drama Academy at Oxford and the Neighborhood Playhouse. She is a member of the New York State Bar, Actor's Equity Association, and the Screen Actor's Guild.

Sherman is a keynote speaker and provides training programs to explore THE EDGE™ for networking, communications, and presentations. She and "the husband" live in Pittsford, NY along with their two children, Zach and Eliza.

www.suburbanoutlaw.com

www.shermanedge.com

CPSIA information can be obtained at www.ICGtesting.com
Printed in the USA
BVOW040601270912

301404BV00007B/2/P